P9-CEX-718

His Choice

A Family's Struggle During Genocide

Angel Nalbandian Rossi
& Susan Parks

Cover design by Hannah Cramer.
Cover photograph by Adam Jones, Ph.D./Flickr.
All scripture quotations are taken from the Holy Bible, *King James Version*

ISBN: 978-1-4497-5830-1 (e)
ISBN: 978-1-4497-5831-8 (sc)
ISBN: 978-1-4497-5832-5 (hc)

Library of Congress Control Number: 2012911980

WestBow Press books may be ordered through booksellers or by contacting:

WestBow Press
A Division of Thomas Nelson
1663 Liberty Drive
Bloomington, IN 47403
www.westbowpress.com
1-(866) 928-1240

Printed in the United States of America

WestBow Press rev. date: 09/10/12

Dedicated to the memory of Paul Kerbajian who was martyred for his faith in Jesus Christ

Acknowledgements

First and foremost, I would like to thank my dear mother, Satenig, who was my inspiration for writing this book. As a young girl, I would sit and listen to my mother and my three aunts talk about the Armenian genocide and the horror they endured. I know you're in heaven, Mom, because *you* are truly my angel.

I am especially thankful to my husband, Al, for his ongoing love and support during this long, and at times, emotional writing process. I appreciate all your encouragement and sage advice during these last five years.

A special thanks to my wonderful son, Albert, who has always been an encouragement to me and most importantly for leading our family to the Lord. Where would we all be today without Christ in our lives!

And of course, a big thank you to my daughter, Susan, who has been such a huge support and encouragement throughout this long undertaking. She is a blessing to our family. Susan, you are my dearest and *very* best friend!

It has been a privilege to work with everyone at Westbow Press. Thank you for all your help and guidance throughout the publishing process.

And finally, I thank the Lord for His wisdom and direction in writing this book.

Angel Nalbandian Rossi

I would like to take this opportunity to express my deepest gratitude to my mother, who has been solely responsible for the successful completion of this book. It would not have been possible without her perseverance and faithfulness. Thank you for being an inspiration to me throughout my life. You're an amazing mother and woman!

I also want to express my sincere gratitude to my husband, Eric, for his love, support and patience during the many years it took to write this book. I am thankful for your encouragement, great wisdom and valuable advice. You are the love of my life and I am blessed to have such a wonderful husband.

An honorable mention goes to my Dad and my brother, Albert, who provided great support during the writing of this book. Thank you for your patience and love.

And finally, I wish to express my love and gratitude to my sons, Brad and Scott and my daughter-in-laws, Sarah and Morgan, for their unending love, support and encouragement. I am most blessed to have such an incredible family.

Thank you to all the great people at Westbow Press, who patiently helped the publishing process go smoothly.

And a very special thank you to Hannah Cramer, graphic designer at Monclova Road Baptist Church. Her beautiful depiction of the book is inspirational.

And most importantly, I am forever thankful to God, who is the author and finisher of our faith.

Susan Parks

Contents

Chapter 1
1965

THE ROSS FAMILY WAS HALFWAY to their destination when Albert shouted from the back seat.

"Wow, look at that huge rain cloud up ahead!"

"I've never seen the sky change so quickly!" Linda said to her brother.

Mom and Dad looked above at the ominous clouds. The bumper-to-bumper traffic on the Long Island Expressway had slowed down, and at times, it came to a complete standstill.

Suddenly, the winds kicked up and were so forceful that the car began to shake and the visibility dropped to near zero. Dad firmly held onto the wheel of their Chevrolet Belair. The children quickly covered their faces as some stones hit the car and dirt pummeled the windows.

Dad put on his emergency lights and pulled off to the shoulder of the road. The change in the weather had created havoc for the families who were travelling on Thanksgiving Day.

The family had to wait for almost an hour for the storm to subside.

"How much longer will we be sitting here in traffic?" Linda asked.

"Yeh, this is really boring and I want to get to Grandma and Grandpa's house!" her brother complained.

"The weather seems to be improving" Mom said.

"Yes, and traffic is gradually starting to move," Dad added.

They continued their drive toward Queens, a borough of New York City. The children were filled with anticipation as they looked forward to seeing their relatives. It was a tradition to gather everyone together at Grandma and Grandpa Nalbandian's house to share in a huge dinner and celebration. Many drove from long distances throughout the New York metropolitan area to reconnect with their immediate and extended Armenian family.

"I hope Grandpa is not too concerned about us. You know how anxious he gets until everyone has arrived safely." Linda remarked.

"Yes, that's your Grandpa Paul! We can usually see him pacing near the front door while waiting for his guests."

"He certainly does his share of worrying for his family! I guess some things never change. He was like that when I was a little girl," Mom smiled.

Albert shouted excitedly, "Dad, are we almost there?"

"We should be there in less than ten minutes, son," he replied.

Finally, the family drove down a street where the homes were attached together like paper dolls. Grandma Satenig and Grandpa Paul lived in a two-story brick house at the end of the block. Their house could easily be seen by the green-and-white-striped canvas awning that covered the front porch.

After they walked up the steps, Dad lifted the heavy brass knocker and rapped on the door.

It swung open, and Grandpa greeted them with a big hug.

"We were beginning to worry about you," he said. "Is everything all right?"

"Oh, we are all fine. We hit a terrible storm which delayed us for almost an hour. The children were somewhat restless, but thankfully, we made it without any mishaps," Mom replied, breathing a sigh of relief.

"Well, come inside and warm up. Dinner is almost ready."

Grandpa put his arms around Albert and Linda and led the children into the living room.

As soon as they entered the house, they could smell the wonderful aroma of the feast that was being prepared. After many hugs and kisses from aunts, uncles, and cousins, they removed their coats. Grandma and Grandpa had been blessed with three children and seven grandchildren.

Mom brushed back her dark hair as she carried a dessert into Grandma's tiny yellow kitchen.

"You asked me to bring my apple crumb pie, so here it is!"

"Oh, that looks delicious, sweetheart. Just set it down on the table with the other desserts," Satenig said to her daughter.

As she entered the room, Mom saw her aunts working side by side, busily cooking and baking their favorite Armenian foods.

She laughed, "It's a good thing you are so slight, or it would be impossible for all of you to work in this tiny kitchen at the same time."

Satenig was the eldest of the four Kerbajian sisters, followed by Yestair, Aznif, and Baizar. The women were humming Armenian songs as they worked.

Aznif was making sarma, the stuffed grape leaves that everyone loved. She placed a mixture of ground beef, rice, chopped tomatoes, and allspice on top of a grape leaf which she then rolled tightly and put into a large pot. After she added some tomato sauce and lemon juice, she placed a plate over the sarma, covered it with a lid, and let it simmer on the stove until it was fork-tender.

Yestair and Baizar were making rice pilaf and Armenian pita bread, while Satenig was basting a large turkey in the oven.

Satenig's eldest daughter, Agnes, walked into the kitchen and asked, "How do you have the patience to make so many sarma rolls, Aunt Aznif? I could never do that."

Agnes's brother, Edward, overheard her comment and yelled from the living room.

"You can say that again, Sis!"

"I have been making these for many years. I like working with my hands, and I enjoy cooking. It's a lot of work, but it's a real blessing to be able to cook for my wonderful family," Aznif said with a warm smile.

The large oval dining room table was set with tall, gleaming water goblets and Grandma's best porcelain dishes which she used only for special occasions. As everyone gathered around the table, Grandma and her three sisters brought in the family's favorite dishes. Grandpa carried the large turkey into the dining room and placed the bird in the center of the table.

"Okay, let's eat," Cousin Robert said. "We're all starving Armenians!"

"Don't joke like that!" Baizar said. "I fail to see the humor in that remark!"

Agnes' twelve year old son was embarrassed as he lowered his head and mumbled an apology.

When everyone was seated, Grandpa began to pray, giving thanks for the food, the gathering of the family, and the freedom that they enjoyed in America. Linda, who was sitting next to her Aunt Aznif, noticed tears in her aunt's eyes and wondered what was wrong.

For many years, Aznif had lived with her sister, Satenig, and her brother-in-law, Paul. She was a quiet woman who had never married but who always helped wherever or whenever she was needed. Her hands were constantly busy. Even when she was relaxing, Aznif was either tatting elegant doilies or knitting sweaters for the children.

Aznif had blue tattoo marks on her face, hands, and knees, and a cross was carved into her cheek. She was very self-conscious about the deep gashes on her shoulder and arm. She always wore calf-length dresses with long sleeves in an effort to cover her disfiguring scars.

Yestair turned to her son, Armen, and said, "Let's take some pictures of the family and the delicious spread of food on the table before us."

Armen slapped his hand to his forehead. "Oh, no, I left my camera at the studio," he said.

Armen, who owned a photography business in Manhattan, designed layouts for advertisements in fashion magazines. Therefore, he was the designated photographer for the family gatherings.

"Don't fret, Mom. Christmas is only a month away, and I'll be sure to bring my camera for our next holiday get-together," he said.

"Well, I hope everyone enjoys the meal," Grandma announced. "A lot of love and care went into its preparation."

She turned to her son, Edward, and said, "I know you wanted to take us out to eat in a restroom, but isn't this better than a restroom?"

Everyone in the family burst into laughter.

Tilting her head to the side, Grandma frowned and asked, "Why are you laughing?"

With a slight grin on his face, Albert said, "Grandma, we always tell you the word is pronounced *restaurant*, not *restroom*!"

Grandma shrugged her shoulders and replied, "What's the difference?"

Once again, the room was filled with laughter.

As soon as they had finished dinner, Albert excused himself and asked, "Does anyone want to play the Twister game with me?" His cousins quickly joined him in the living room.

The boys eagerly began to play the game, and within minutes, their boisterous shouts and laughter filled the room. The four cousins were having a great time. A loud cheer went up, and as he had predicted, Albert, who was very quick and agile, had won the game.

Young Jackie, who was sitting next to her great aunt in the dining room, asked, "Aunt Aznif, why were you crying when Grandpa prayed at the dinner table?"

Aunt Aznif thought for a moment and softly answered, "These past ten years have been the happiest years of my life. I am reminded that every day is a gift from God. I'm just so thankful to be here with my wonderful family; a family that I didn't even know existed until twelve years ago."

She dabbed at her eyes with her napkin as tears rolled down her scarred and wrinkled face.

Grandma Satenig thought for a moment and quietly interjected, “It is very difficult for us to talk about our past. It brings back so many painful memories. It’s not only one day that we give thanks to God. We, Kerbajian sisters, are thankful every day of our lives for the Lord watching over us and bringing us through the genocide. Each of us had our own personal difficulties during that terrible time. It is a miracle that we are all together at last,” Satenig explained.

The sisters began to talk about the years during the genocide.

Yestir, took a deep breath, slowly turned and looked at her niece, Jackie.

“Let me try to explain what happened in April of 1915,” Yestair said.

The sisters leaned toward one another, with their knees almost touching, as Jackie and her cousins settled into the corner of the couch. The two youngest boys slipped into the living room and sat cross-legged on the floor behind the couch, hoping the older women wouldn’t shoo them away.

The rest of the family gathered around the four sisters as they talked about their travails during the Armenian genocide. They started to share their harrowing and life-threatening experiences, and had to stop several times in order to catch their breath and wipe the tears from their faces.

Chapter 2

Family Life

"MAMA, I FELL DOWN AND my mouth is bleeding. I think I may have knocked out some of my teeth!" young Aram mumbled.

Engrossed in her food preparations, Mama turned around and shouted, "How did this happen? Where is your father?"

"Paul, come quickly. Aram is bleeding!"

Aram's younger sisters, Aznif and Baizar heard the commotion coming from the kitchen.

Aznif had been watching over her energetic younger sister, Baizar, while Mama was making dinner.

"Shh, be really quiet," whispered the four year old.

Baizar had the living room door ajar and was peeking into the kitchen.

"Mama and Papa would be disappointed if they knew that you were snooping on them," Aznif said.

As the youngest sibling, Baizar had a skillful way of influencing her more compliant older sister.

"Oh, look at Aram. Come over here, Aznif, as she motioned with her hand. This is really funny!"

Aznif tried holding back but her curiosity got the best of her and she gave into her sister's request.

When they sneaked a peek, they saw that Aram had a slice of pomegranate between his upper and lower lip. He bit down hard on the fruit, causing the crimson juice to dribble down his chin.

They snickered at one another, trying to stifle their laughter as they watched their brother's mischievous behavior.

Papa rushed into the kitchen and saw what his son was up to.

"Aram, you almost scared your Mama half to death!"

"Now, young man, you will not be allowed to play with your sisters for the rest of the day, and you are not going up to the roof to play with your friends!"

"But Papa, I—"

"Don't talk back to me. Now you go and apologize to your poor mother!"

"Papa, I was only playing a little joke,"the eight year old muttered. He lowered his head and slowly walked into the kitchen.

"Mama, I'm very sorry. I didn't mean to scare you."

The teary-eyed little boy hugged his mother and said he would never do that again.

"Mama, Papa. Is anyone home?" Satenig yelled from the front door.

Satenig and Yestir had just returned from the local market in town. The two girls had the weekly responsibility of shopping for groceries and they were laden with many bags of food.

They walked into their house which was usually filled with excitement, but noticed it was strangely quiet.

"Where are Mama and Papa? They always help us with the groceries." Yestir remarked to Satenig.

Aznif and Baizar heard their sisters talking. They greeted the girls and immediately told them what had just happened.

Twelve year old Satenig was upset when she heard about Aram's prank on Mama. Yestair shook her head back and forth as she listened closely to her younger sisters.

The Kerbajian family lived in a small village near the foothills of Mount Ararat, the place where Noah's Ark came to rest. The ancient snowcapped mountain was the symbol of their Christian religion.

Papa was a schoolteacher and a well-known artist. Although he enjoyed teaching, his true passion was his art. He often traveled to nearby towns and villages to paint murals on the walls of the Armenian churches. His depiction of Jesus on the cross was so realistic and moving that people often wept when they looked at the heart-wrenching scene. Papa worked tirelessly at his craft and served the Lord with joy.

Mama was a warm and loving nurturer. With five young children to care for, she was always busy providing her family with all the necessities they needed for a healthy, balanced life. She was a role model for her four daughters as she taught them basic homemaking skills.

Papa taught Aram, their only son, the many skills that he would need in order to provide for his future family. Papa emphasized the importance of being conscientious and having a good work ethic. Mama and Papa taught their children Christian values and raised their family with Christ as the center of their lives. How blessed the children were to have such concerned and wonderful parents.

The Kerbajians lived in a house built of sandstone. The homes in their village were connected with adjoining flat roofs. Each family's house had an attached ladder behind it which provided easy access to the roof. On warm, summer nights, the family would climb up the ladder and socialize with their neighbors while they enjoyed the cool evening breeze. The children had fun playing games and running from one roof to the next with their Armenian and Turkish friends.

The family lived peacefully with their Turkish neighbors. Although their religious beliefs were extremely different, their daily lives were alike in many ways. The foods they ate, the games they played, and the music that they listened to were very similar.

The living room was the hub of their family's life. During the cold winter months, they would gather around the *toneer*, which was a round stone fireplace in the center of the room, in which a fire continually burned. The toneer supplied heat for the home and was also used to cook many of the family's meals.

Every night after dinner the children looked forward to family time. Mama usually prepared a tray of nuts, pomegranates, pita bread, and madzoon (yogurt) for their evening snack. The children's favorite fruit was pomegranate. Mama would slice a bright red pomegranate into quarters, which they would then eat like an orange.

Everyone warmed their feet around the fireplace and shared the events of their day. The family also spent time reading the Bible and praying together. Family time was a very special time that they often took for granted, never realizing how drastically their lives would change in a very short time.

One night, Mama announced that her unmarried brother, Jim Chunkalian, was on furlough and would be coming to stay with them for a few days. Uncle Jim was a general in the Armenian Army, and the children loved him and were very excited to see him. He was always full of fun and regaled them with stories about army life. The children loved his quick wit and keen sense of humor.

"Oh, I can't wait to see Uncle Jim. I want to be just like him, when I grow up," Aram firmly stated.

The day had finally arrived. Papa saw Uncle Jim riding up to the house, on his horse, Hunter.

Papa ran into the house and called, "Children, come outside and say hello to your uncle."

The children quickly ran out and looked in awe at Uncle Jim sitting on his beautiful Arabian stallion. The huge horse was dark brown and had a black tail and a black mane which ran down his long, arched neck.

When the children walked near the horse, Hunter quickly turned his head and stared at them. His large brown eyes darted back and forth nervously.

"Please don't get too close to the horse" Uncle Jim warned the children.

"He is a highly sensitive animal and it would be wise to keep your distance until the horse gets used to everyone."

Mama suggested that everyone go inside and get ready for dinner. Papa and Uncle Jim fed the horse some oats and gave the thirsty animal a large pail of water to drink. After he tied Hunter to the porch railing, Uncle Jim removed the heavy saddle off the horse's back. Everyone then went inside, washed their hands, and sat down at the dinner table.

"Uncle Jim, do you have any good stories to tell us?" Aram asked excitedly.

As she placed her hand on her son's arm, Mama said, "Let your uncle relax, son. I'm sure he is very tired from the long trip."

"But Mama, Uncle Jim is a soldier, and soldiers *never* get tired!"

Uncle Jim laughed and replied, "Sorry to disappoint you, Aram, but soldiers *do* get tired!"

"Why don't we eat first and then later I'll tell you some stories, okay?"

They sat down to a sumptuous meal of leg of lamb, rice pilaf, and okra stew. After they had coffee and pahklava for dessert, Uncle Jim asked his nephew, "Now what do you want to know, my little man?"

"Uncle Jim, what is it like to be a general?" Aram asked.

"Well, it's a lot of hard work, and it is a big responsibility to strategically plan and lead soldiers into battle with a minimal amount of casualties. But, Aram, it is an honor to serve and protect our people."

Uncle Jim was a strong man. He appeared taller than he actually was because of his broad shoulders and erect posture. He had a noticeable white scar that ran from his left ear down to his chin. Jim Chunkalian was known as a brilliant strategist and was well respected and admired for his bravery.

After dinner, Uncle Jim asked, "Does anyone want to take a ride on my horse?"

Satenig's hand was the first one that went up. She was the most adventurous of the children and loved a new challenge.

"Are you sure you want to do this?" her uncle asked.

Satenig quickly nodded her head.

"Okay, let's go outside and get Hunter ready."

"I don't think this is a good idea. Your horse is much too strong and powerful for a young girl's first ride on a horse," Mama interjected.

Her free-spirited brother shook his head and said, "I have full control over my horse. He is a well-trained animal. You don't have to worry about anything."

Satenig seemed apprehensive as she looked up at the huge horse. She had not realized how powerful this horse was and how tiny she felt when she stood next to him.

Interlocking his hands, Uncle Jim instructed Satenig, "Now place your foot in my hand, and I'll boost you up onto Hunter. Then I'll climb up behind you, and we will ride together."

In a moment, Satenig found herself sitting high on top of the massive animal. Uncle Jim mounted Hunter, and they took off.

"Oh, this is such fun!" Satenig squealed as she bounced up and down in the saddle.

Suddenly, Hunter turned his head, snorted loudly, and began to race down the road. Uncle Jim ordered the horse to slow down, but the animal was spooked and ran even faster. What began as an adventure almost ended in tragedy as Uncle Jim tried to bring the animal to a halt.

Uncle Jim found it difficult to control the frightened horse while he was holding onto his terrified niece at the same time. He pulled tightly on the reins as he shouted and ordered the horse to stop.

Finally, after several harrowing minutes, Hunter slowed down, and Uncle Jim breathed a sigh of relief. He saw that his niece was sobbing and breathing heavily. He turned the animal around and slowly led the horse back to the house.

When they reached the railing, Jim tied the horse securely to the post and gently lifted his traumatized niece off Hunter's back. He gave his niece a big hug, reassuring her that everything was all right. She was in a state of shock, and her heart was still beating rapidly.

Trying to make light of the situation, Uncle Jim said, "Now that was an exciting adventure, wasn't it, Satenig?"

"*No!* I was so scared. I hate that nasty horse! Don't you ever again put me on him!"

"Horses are highly sensitive animals, especially Arabian stallions. When you were laughing and bouncing up and down in the saddle, the horse was not used to that and he became frightened," Uncle Jim calmly explained.

Although he was concerned about what could have happened, he smiled and gave Satenig another hug.

She pulled away and said, "Well, I'm glad he was afraid. I will never ride on that horse again!" Satenig rubbed her eyes with the back of her hands.

Uncle Jim gave a sigh of relief and whispered a prayer of thanksgiving to God for protecting his precious niece from injury.

Uncle Jim stayed with the family for a few days and then left early one morning. The children loved listening to his fascinating adventures and were sorry that he had to leave. He climbed upon Hunter, waved, and said he would see them again very soon.

Sadly, that was the last time they saw their beloved uncle.

Chapter 3

Paul and Ahmed

PAUL WAS ON HIS WAY to work one morning when he saw his Turkish friend, Ahmed, who indicated with a wave of his hand that he wanted to speak to him. Paul crossed the street to meet his old friend and extended his hand to Ahmed. The two men warmly greeted one another with a handshake and a hug.

Paul and Ahmed had been good friends since they were children, competing in games, sharing stories, and playing jokes on one another. Ahmed had a keen sense of humor, and the more serious Paul was a perfect foil for his many jokes.

At the age of thirty-five, Ahmed held an important position in the Turkish government. He was a tall, lanky man with intense brown eyes. As always, he was impeccably groomed and looked very distinguished in a three-piece black suit. On his head, he wore a traditional maroon fez with a black tassel on one side.

"Do you have a few moments to spare, Paul?" asked Ahmed. "I would like to talk to you."

Cocking his head to one side, Paul replied, "Sure, we haven't had much time to visit lately since we both have such busy schedules."

"Why don't we go to that café across the street and have a cup of coffee," Ahmed suggested.

The two friends began to walk toward a row of small shops. When they arrived at the café, they entered the crowded restaurant and found a table in the back of the room. Ahmed ordered two cups of the strong

Turkish coffee that they both liked. The waiter set the small cups down on the table.

"Is there anything else I can get for you, gentlemen?" he asked.

"Would you like something to eat, my friend?" Ahmed asked Paul.

As he patted his stomach, Paul laughed. "No thank you, Ahmed. I just had a huge breakfast a short while ago."

Ahmed replied, "I haven't had a chance to eat breakfast this morning."

He turned to the waiter and said, "I'd like to order some fresh pita bread and a serving of Armenian string cheese."

As he was eating, Paul noticed that Ahmed appeared uneasy. His face was tense, and he seemed worried. Ahmed was unlike his usual jovial self.

"How are you and your family doing? I hope everyone is well," Paul asked.

"Oh, we're fine, Paul. How are your wife and children? We haven't seen them in quite a while. Perhaps you and your family can join us for dinner sometime soon. The children have so much fun when they get together."

"Everyone is well, and yes, we would love to come for dinner. Let the women decide on a convenient time and day. We will look forward to it." Paul paused and looked at his friend. "Are you okay, *effendi*? You look a little tired."

"As a matter of fact, I am rather fatigued because of the many long hours that I have been spending at the office," Ahmed replied.

After he leaned closer, Ahmed whispered, "Paul, I need to talk to you about an extremely important matter."

As he looked around the restaurant, he said, "Let's finish our coffee and take a walk outside for a while. It's a little noisy in here."

The two men chatted and walked for a few blocks until they came to a small park. Ahmed led Paul to a secluded area near a copse of cedar trees. He pointed to a bench and the men sat down and relaxed for a few moments.

"This is so much better. It's cool and pleasant under this tree, isn't it, Paul?" Ahmed said as he removed the fez from his head and placed it on the bench.

Ahmed leaned toward Paul and whispered, "I recently attended a meeting with the Committee of Union and Progress. The acronym for this committee is the CUP. It was a very disturbing meeting, and it could possibly affect you and your family."

Startled by what Ahmed said, Paul asked, "What do you mean? Why would this affect my family and me?"

"Let me try to explain to you what has been transpiring at the CUP meetings."

Ahmed cleared his throat. He placed his arm on the back of the bench in an attempt to appear relaxed.

"Do you remember what happened in Adana in 1909, Paul?"

"No, maybe you can refresh my memory. I don't know where this conversation is going," Paul answered.

"Let me give you some background about what occurred at that time. Adana was a very prosperous town near the Mediterranean Sea. The Armenians owned the majority of the businesses there. They were ambitious and hardworking, and they enjoyed a very high standard of living. The Muslim Turks hated the 'infidels' and their God."

"The newly formed Committee of Union and Progress devised a plan to get rid of the wealthy Armenian merchants. This was to be carried out by a group called the 'Young Turks' who had the reputation of being ruthless killers."

Ahmed paused and cleared his throat. "When you hear the results of this terrible plan, perhaps you will understand what I am attempting to tell you.

"I still do not understand what this has to do with me. I am neither a wealthy man nor a merchant, Ahmed," Paul replied.

Holding up his hand, Ahmed answered, "I know that, but please, Paul, hear me out. In the beginning, the Young Turks began looting the stores. Eventually, they shot the store owners. In defense, the Armenian merchants fired back in order to protect their property. This escalated into complete havoc. The Young Turks raided several Armenian quarters all day and throughout the night. Within a few days, over two thousand Armenians were slaughtered. Then all businesses, schools, and churches were burned to the ground. Eventually, the Young Turks continued on a rampage and went from town to town, demolishing everything and everyone in sight. In the end, over two hundred villages and towns were razed, and an estimated twenty-three thousand Armenians were massacred. They deliberately killed all the young adult males so they could not procreate. Do you now understand the intentions of the CUP committee?"

"That happened six years ago!" Paul said.

"Since then, nothing like that has occurred in our area. We do not have any problems like that here in Eastern Turkey. We get along fairly well with one another. Of course, at times, we disagree on certain issues, but we settle our disputes amicably."

Paul was silent and he slowly shook his head back and forth. He was trying to understand what Ahmed was telling him. He was horrified by the news and was filled with fear for his wife and five children.

"Paul, you seem upset, as well you should be. But listen, my friend. I am very concerned for the safety of you and your family. We have been the best of friends for over twenty-five years, and I would be remiss if I didn't inform you of their strategy."

"The CUP is planning to get rid of all the Armenians living in Turkey!"

"Paul, please listen to me! I am taking a very big risk by telling you about this, but in all good consciousness, I feel I must warn you. Time is of the essence, and you must start making plans for yourself and your loved ones."

"Have you seen the notices that have been posted in the village? It says that all Armenians must surrender any weapons that they have in their possession to police headquarters."

"Yes, I have seen the notices, but I don't understand why they would want us to do that. I have also heard that if anyone disobeys this order, they will be arrested. Is this true, or is it just another rumor going around, Ahmed?" Paul raked his fingers through his hair.

He took a deep breath and sighed. "Why would they take away our weapons and leave us completely defenseless? That doesn't make sense!"

Shaking his head back and forth, with a slight smirk on his face, Ahmed replied, "It makes *perfect* sense. It is part of their well-calculated and systematic plan. When the Armenian shop owners in Adana began to shoot back at the looters and murderers, the government decided to confiscate all weapons from the Armenians to prevent the Young Turks from being killed."

"The ultimate goal is to have Turkey become a nation of people who speak the same language and who have the same religion. Understand that the government will stop at nothing until every Christian Armenian is either deported or killed! Do you understand *now*, Paul?"

"I know there has been some talk and speculation about these notices, but I never realized the magnitude of this growing hatred for the Armenians. I am shocked to hear all this, to say the least," Paul responded sadly.

"Paul, the first group to be arrested and possibly killed will be the professional and intellectual people, such as lawyers, doctors, teachers, and government officials. Since you are a teacher, as well as an artist in the Armenian churches, I feel I must explain the severity of this situation. Listen, my friend. I have an idea that may help you."

Ahmed leaned closer to Paul. "You are a very talented man. You and your family can be saved from this oncoming annihilation."

"Can I ask you a question, Paul?"

"Of course, what do you want to know, Ahmed?"

"I have really been thinking about this situation a great deal. I am very concerned for the welfare of you and your family."

Looking intently at Paul, he asked, "Would you consider painting in our mosques?"

Shocked by Ahmed's question, Paul replied, "Ahmed, you know that I paint and do some sculpting in our Armenian churches and in our ancient cathedrals. As a matter of fact, I am in the middle of carving a stone *khatch* (cross) into the outer wall of the new church in a nearby village. How could I, a Christian, possibly paint in a Muslim mosque?"

"Well, you would have to convert to the Islamic religion," Ahmed flippantly replied.

Paul shook his head back and forth and answered, "I will *never* give up my Christianity!"

"I would rather die than denounce my beliefs! How can you even suggest that I convert?"

"I know how strong you are in your convictions, and believe me, I respect you for that, Paul, but you must think of your family. Have you considered what could possibly happen to your wife and five children? This is going to be a deadly attack on all Armenian Christians."

"Please discuss our conversation with your wife. And perhaps she will be more reasonable, and we can come to a sensible solution to this problem. This is a life-threatening situation, and you will not heed my warning!"

"Don't you realize that I am trying to help you? Listen to me, Paul. You know that we've been friends since childhood, and that I would never steer you wrong."

"Ahmed, I truly appreciate your concern for me and my family, but you must understand that I am a Christian, and I shall remain a Christian no matter what happens," Paul firmly replied.

Ahmed closed his eyes and slowly shook his head back and forth.

"I don't know what to say except I hope your God will be with you and your family in the coming weeks. You are an intelligent man, nevertheless a very foolish one, and you will rue this day. If you change your mind, you know where to contact me."

"Good luck, my friend."

Paul and Ahmed shook hands, and each man went their separate ways.

Chapter 4

The Anniversary

"Mama, may I go outside and play ball with my friend Peter?" Aram asked.

"Yes, but don't go far, Aram," Mama warned. "Papa will soon be home for dinner."

Aram grabbed his ball. "Okay, I'll come home as soon as you call me."

Aram was an obedient boy, and he was very much loved by his four sisters. He was a happy-go-lucky child who usually had a big smile on his face. He loved a good laugh and enjoyed playing jokes on his more serious siblings.

Satenig, Yestair, and Baizar were helping their mother prepare dinner. Satenig was cutting lamb and vegetables into chunks for shish kebab. Yestair was kneading the dough to make bread for their evening meal.

"Every Armenian girl must learn how to make pahklava. Now that you are six years old, Aznif, you are old enough to learn how to make our favorite dessert. Come here, sweetheart, and stand beside me. You can watch how I butter each sheet of dough," her mother said.

Aznif watched her mother brush some melted butter on the paper-thin dough. She repeated the process with five more layers and then sprinkled a mixture of chopped walnuts, sugar, and cinnamon on top of the phyllo dough.

"Now you must carefully place a sheet of dough on top of the nut mixture," her mother instructed.

Aznif picked up the delicate phyllo dough, which immediately tore and fell apart in her hands.

"I can't do this, Mama. I ruined the pahklava!"

"No, you didn't ruin it. I remember when I was learning how to make pahklava. It took a lot of time and patience to learn how to handle such fragile dough. Now let's try it again."

Following her mother's instruction, Aznif was excited when she successfully handled the dough without tearing it. Aznif loved her mother and she always tried to please her. She was amazed at how patient her mother was with her and also with her brother and sisters. She hoped that someday she would be a kind and loving mother like her mother was to her children.

Zabel smiled at her daughter. She proceeded to cut the dessert into diamond-shaped pieces.

Then she slid the baking pan into the oven and called to Satenig, "Please check to see if the cheoreg dough is ready to be rolled out."

"Shall I remove the towel from around the stone crock now?" Satenig asked.

Mama nodded and looked into the pot. She saw that the dough was ready to be formed into various shapes. She always made a deep imprint in the center of the raw dough by holding her fingers together and pressing them into the dough, marking it with a large cross.

"Why do you always make a cross in the cheoreg dough?" Baizar asked.

Her mother explained, "When we can no longer see the indentation of the cross, we know that the dough has risen and is ready to be rolled out."

Satenig took the cover off the pot and saw a mound of puffy dough. She knew the cheoreg was ready to be rolled out. The delicious aroma of the coriander and mahleb spices that were mixed into the dough permeated the kitchen.

Satenig sprinkled some flour on the table, and each girl pulled off a piece of dough and began forming it into braids and circles. After they carefully brushed each biscuit with an egg wash, they placed it on a baking sheet and slid it into the oven.

Just then Aram ran into the kitchen. He noticed that his sisters were molding the cheoreg into several different shapes.

"Why didn't you call me inside to help you make the cheoreg?" he cried.

"We have just started, and there is plenty of dough to roll out. Now if you go and wash your hands, you may help us," Yestair said.

Aram quickly washed up and then began to roll the dough into a long rope. He was deep in concentration as he pulled and stretched the dough into various shapes.

"Mama, look what I made!" Aram held up a lopsided "A" and the letter "K."

"What is that? Why are you playing with the dough?" Mama reprimanded.

"I'm not playing, Mama. I just invented something. Look, these are my initials. Isn't that clever? Now no one will eat my cheoreg because they will know that it's mine. How is *that!*"

Mama started to laugh. "That's very creative. You are artistic just like your Papa."

Aram grinned. "Yes, I am *very* talented. Just wait until Papa sees my personalized cheoreg. He will love it! Please put my bread in the oven. I can't wait to see how it looks when it is baked."

Papa opened the front door and took a deep breath. *Oh, something smells good. It's making my stomach growl*, he thought to himself.

"Hello, I'm home. Where is everybody?"

Papa walked into the kitchen and smiled at his family, who were busy with their baking.

Aram ran to his father. "Wait until you see what your talented son has made!

"After dinner, I will show you my newest creation, okay? You know, Papa, I've been thinking—"

"Oh, no, you're not thinking again, are you, son?" Papa said with a laugh.

"Please, Papa, don't make fun. This is very serious. I have decided to be an inventor when I grow up. I have so many ideas in my head, and I know I can create some things that will help other people. What do you think about that?"

Papa laughed. "That sounds wonderful. We'll talk about your future career later, okay?"

Aram smiled and nodded his head and went into the dining room.

"Before we sit down to eat, I have a surprise for you, Zabel, my dear."

"Fifteen years ago today, you made me the happiest man on earth. Happy Anniversary, Sweetheart."

Papa reminisced about the day. "Your mother was such a beautiful bride."

He spoke of her shyness and how nervous she was on her wedding day.

Mama smiled. "I could not believe I was about to marry the handsome and talented Paul Kerbajian. Naturally, I was nervous. I was only eighteen years old, and I was about to marry an older man of twenty-two," she said with a laugh.

Paul reached into his pocket and handed his wife a small satin pouch with a drawstring. Zabel's heart melted when she opened the pouch and saw a pair of pink tourmaline and rose-cut diamond earrings.

Her eyes filled with tears. "Oh, they are so beautiful, Paul. Thank you so much."

She leaned over and kissed him on the cheek. "I'm so sorry. I forgot that today was our anniversary. I don't know where my mind is lately."

Aram looked and pointed to his parents and cried out, "Oh, look at the two lovebirds!" The family laughed at Aram's outburst.

"I'll pass the earrings around the table so everyone can see them. Be careful not to drop them. They are fragile and very precious," Mama said.

The girls *oohed* and *aahed* as they admired the earrings. Aznif tried them on.

"Oh, let me see them!" Aram screeched, imitating his sisters' excitement.

"Okay, settle down, children. Let's begin to eat this wonderful dinner that your mother has prepared for us."

After dinner, Paul got up and sat in his favorite chair and looked outside the window. He was deep in thought and seemed to be worried about something.

"Is Papa feeling all right?" Satenig asked her mother. Satenig, being the eldest child, was always concerned about the welfare of her parents and her siblings. If there was a problem in the house, she was always there to help in any way that she could.

"Oh, he's fine," Mama said. "He probably had a busy day at work."

"Now that we've finished eating, you children may go out and play for a while before it turns dark."

When the children left, Paul patted the seat next to him. "Come here, dear. I have something I want to discuss with you."

"Is there anything wrong, Paul? You're not acting like yourself. *Eench-eh*?" (What is it?)

"I saw Ahmed this morning, and he gave me some troubling information about a plan that the Turkish government has devised."

Paul leaned toward his wife and whispered, "They plan to systematically annihilate all Armenian Christians who are living in Turkey."

Zabel gasped and put her hands over her mouth.

Paul sighed. "The first group to be arrested will most likely be the professionals. He mentioned doctors, lawyers, bankers, teachers, and artisans. Ahmed said that since I am a teacher and an artist working in churches, our family could be in a very vulnerable position".

"He suggested a way that I might avoid being arrested. He wanted me to convert to the Muslim religion and paint in their mosques, which, of course, I refused to do!"

"I feel it is prudent that we prepare provisions in case something happens and we are forced to leave our home."

"I don't understand this, Paul. Why would we have to leave our home? All these years, we have worked hard for what little we have, and we've never had problems with anyone."

Zabel placed her hand over her heart. "Why is it that when everytime things are going well in our lives, something happens and we become worried and upset? There is only one thing that we must do. We must pray for God's direction for our family."

Paul held Zabel's hand and they bowed their heads in prayer.

"What do we say to the children?" Zabel asked worriedly.

"We need to talk to them about this situation, but we must not frighten them," Paul said.

"Please ask them to come in now."

When Mama called the children to come home, Aznif whined, "But it's still light outside. Can't we play a little longer?"

"No, your father and I have something that we want to discuss with you."

The children reluctantly entered the house.

Papa said, "Come here and sit beside me. We have to talk together as a family."

"I don't want to frighten you, but there might be a conflict between the Turks and the Armenians. Your mother and I feel that we should be prepared in case we are asked to leave our home."

"Is there going to be a war, Papa?" Satenig asked.

"I don't think so," he replied, "but it is best to take precautions."

"But Papa, how can we be at war with our friends and neighbors?"

He answered, "I do not think there will be a war, but some families have been forced out of their homes, so we must be prepared just in case this should happen to us."

Papa noticed the troubled look on his children's faces.

"Please don't worry. I just want us to have a plan in place for our peace of mind. We will need food, water, and clothing. I want each of you to gather some clothes and personal items and give them to your mother."

Mama prepared the package of food and water, while the children went to their rooms to get their belongings. She wrapped dried meat, cheoreg, and lavoush bread in towels for easy carrying. She then filled a jug of water and put everything in the back bedroom.

Satenig tried to keep the children calm. Even though she was frightened, she helped her parents and showed the younger children what to do. A shiver went down her spine when she realized that they could possibly be leaving their comfortable home. Where would they go? When would they return to the only home they had ever known?

She turned her head to one side so that the children would not see the tears in her eyes.

Papa entered the room. "We must remember to bring money with us. I'll go and get my strongbox right now while I'm thinking about it."

While he was gathering the money, Zabel took out her jewelry and wrapped the few pieces she owned in a soft cloth. Paul came into the bedroom, carrying his strongbox.

"Do you think it would be a good idea if I sew the money and jewelry into the hem of our skirts?" Zabel said. "This way, no one will see us carrying anything of value."

"I think that's a great idea. You always were the clever one in this family!"

"Oh, I hardly think so. You are the one who is multitalented and a man who always thinks of his family's safety and well-being."

Zabel then leaned over to receive her husband's affectionate kiss.

Zabel placed all of their money and her jewels in the bottom of the skirts. Then she turned up the material and sewed the hems with strong waxed thread. It was so well sewn that no one would ever know that all their savings and valuables were hidden in their clothing. When Zabel finished sewing the hems of the skirts, she looked up and noticed that Aznif was still wearing her new earrings.

"Take the earrings off. I forgot to put the earrings in the skirt."

"All right, Mama," Aznif said.

Before she could take them off, Papa suddenly walked into the room.

"Zabel, have you finished sewing my suit pants? I have an important meeting tomorrow with the pastor of the church."

Mama stopped and said, "I'm sorry, dear. I forgot that your pants needed to be shortened. I'll do it right away."

Mama quickly finished packing the clothes. She placed her Bible on top of the bundle. Then she tied everything in a blanket. She carried it into the bedroom and placed it next to other items.

"Now that we are prepared, it is time to go to bed," she said.

Papa hugged each child, "*Keshare paree* (good night), little ones. Don't forget to say your prayers."

The children nodded, kissed their parents, and went off to bed.

Chapter 5
The Young Turks

THE FOLLOWING DAY, AFTER THE family had their evening meal, Papa asked the children if they had completed their homework.

Since he was a teacher, Papa was always concerned with their education. He would check their papers carefully to make sure that everything was completed and done correctly. He wanted his children to excel in school, and he was meticulous about their work ethic.

After Aram's work had been checked, he asked, "Papa, may I go outside for a little while to play ball?"

His father nodded, and Aram quickly raced out of the house.

A short time later, Paul was startled by a strange sound. He frowned and turned his head as he listened intently to the noise. Paul shrugged his shoulders when he realized that it was just some horses that were racing down the dirt road. Then he heard loud snorting and the stomping of horses' hooves as they came to a halt outside their front door.

Papa looked out of the window and saw four Turkish soldiers who were clad in dark brown military uniforms. They were holding rifles and sabers.

Paul remembered what his friend Ahmed had told him about the plans of the Turkish government. A shiver ran down Paul's spine and was paralyzed with fear for his family.

One of the soldiers who seemed to be in charge, raised his rifle in the air and yelled, "Paul Kerbajian, on behalf of the government, we demand that you come outside, or we will enter and drag you out by force!"

Another soldier screamed, "Turkey is for the Turks!"

Paul immediately knew that they were part of the military group known as the Young Turks that his friend, Ahmed, had told him about a few weeks ago.

After he put a finger to his lips, Paul whispered to his wife, "Listen to me. If anything happens, remember the plan we made. Take the children to the back of the house and quickly gather the provisions that we have prepared. Then run as fast as you can and hide in the woods behind the house."

Zabel was frozen with fear. She grabbed hold of her husband's arm and pleaded, "Please . . . don't open the door! I'm so afraid, Paul! *Eench-gooz-een*? (What do they want?)"

"Please, Zabel, for the sake of the children, try to remain calm while I find out what this is all about."

Paul opened the door and walked outside, firmly closing the door behind him. Although he showed great courage, Paul had a premonition of impending doom.

Trying to keep himself under control, he spoke to the officer.

"There must be some mistake here. I have done nothing wrong. What is it you want from me?"

The soldier in charge harshly replied, "Do you have any guns in your house? I'm sure you are well aware that we have orders to collect weapons from all Armenians. I have a list of everyone in the village who has surrendered their weapons to the police, and your name is not on the list. You infidels are a thorn in our country's side!"

The officer tightened the grip on his rifle and glared at Paul. "Answer me now, you dog!"

Shaking his head back and forth, Paul replied, "I do not own any—"

From the corner of his eye, Paul spotted Aram, who was casually playing with his ball down the road. He shouted to him, "Aram, hurry! Run!"

Not understanding what was going on, Aram started to run toward his father. Paul knew that his young son was not aware of the imminent danger ahead. He was in a state of panic, but he knew he had to protect his innocent son from these vicious Young Turks.

As Paul's heart thundered in his chest, he quickly turned away from the soldiers and ran down the road toward his son. He saw the confused and frightened look on Aram's face. Paul knew he had to be with his child in order to comfort and protect his son.

When one of the soldiers saw Paul running away, he quickly mounted his horse and galloped after him. He pulled his curved scimitar from its scabbard, and as he approached the fleeing man, he leaned down from his horse and struck Paul below the chin. Paul's knees buckled beneath him, and he fell to the ground, his head no longer intact.

Aram screamed in horror when he saw the blood pouring out of his father's body.

In shock, he wailed, "Papa, Papa, help me!" He turned to run away, but he was not quick enough. Another soldier rode toward the young boy and pierced his chest with his sword. The boy made a soft mewing sound, and then he was silent.

When Zabel heard the high-pitched scream from her son, she dashed out of the house and ran toward her loved ones. When she saw the carnage before her, she fell to her knees, keening loudly. Covering her eyes with her hands, she screamed hysterically, "*Asvadzim*! *Asvadzim*!" (My God, My God!)

She never saw nor heard the soldier who was racing on his horse toward her. In an instant and with one swift movement of his arm, Zabel met with the same fate as her husband.

For whosoever will save his life shall lose it: But whosoever will lose his life for my sake, the same shall save it.

Luke 9:24

Chapter 6

The Escape

When Satenig did not hear any noise or voices from outside, she carefully pulled a corner of the window curtain aside and looked around. Then she motioned to Yestair that the soldiers were no longer near the house.

Yestair cautiously looked out of the window and saw something odd down the road. She pointed to the bodies lying on the ground. When the two sisters saw the carnage before them, they covered their mouths with their hands to suppress their screams. They did not want to frighten their younger sisters, but they could not stop the tears that were pouring down their shocked faces. Seeing the bloody bodies of their parents and their precious brother lying on the dirt road was too much to bear. They held on to one another for comfort and wailed, but there was no comfort to be had.

Baizar cried, "What's wrong? What's happening? Pick me up! I can't see anything!"

Satenig moved to her baby sister, picked her up, and hugged her tightly to her chest.

"I want Mama. Where is she? I want to go outside!" Baizar screamed.

Satenig silently prayed, "Lord, help me. I don't know what to do! How do I explain this to my sisters? How can I tell the little ones what has happened to our parents and brother? Please give me strength and wisdom, Father."

Then Satenig remembered the instructions that Papa had given to them in case anything happened.

"Let's go to the back bedroom and gather the provisions that Mama and Papa have stored in the closet."

"I don't want to go. I don't have to listen to you. You are not my mother! I am going to stay here and wait for Mama. You can go without me," Baizar cried loudly.

Yestair saw the look of dismay on Satenig's face and knew that she had to do something quickly. "Come with me, Baizar. You and Aznif can help me, okay?" Yestair said to her younger sisters.

"Oh, I am a good helper!" Baizar said excitedly.

Yestair was so relieved that her baby sister knew nothing about the brutal murders of their parents and young brother.

"I know you are, sweetheart. Now let's hurry. We must be very quiet, so please do not speak. Do you understand?"

Yestair put her thumb and forefinger to Baizar's lips and turned them like a key, indicating to her baby sister that they needed to be perfectly quiet.

"Aznif, you hold this small jug of water and take Baizar to the back of the house and help her to climb up the ladder. I will be right behind you. Now hurry!"

Aznif nodded her head and swiftly walked to the back of the house with her baby sister in tow.

Yestair grabbed the food package and quickly climbed up to the roof to join her sisters.

At the same time, Satenig picked up the heavy blanket filled with their clothing. She ran toward the back door. As she closed the door behind her, Satenig knew that this would be the last time she and her sisters would live in this warm and loving home with their wonderful parents. That realization caused her to clutch her heaving chest as she sobbed uncontrollably.

Wiping the tears from her eyes, Satenig reluctantly began her ascent up to the roof.

When they reached the top of the roof, the four terrified sisters ran rapidly across several of the connected roofs. They looked around and saw that there was no sign of any soldiers, so they climbed down the ladder and ran to the woods for safety.

After they ran for a while, they stopped to catch their breath. They had been resting for several minutes when they heard the dreaded sound of horses' hooves.

"Hurry up! Run toward that thick cluster of trees in the back so no one can see us," Satenig whispered.

"Remember, do not speak or make noise of any kind."

As they were running, Yestair heard a loud scream. She turned around and realized that Aznif was not with them. She tapped Satenig on her shoulder. Satenig turned around and saw that Aznif had fallen over a tree limb. To her horror, she saw a soldier racing toward Aznif.

In a split second, he dismounted his horse and struck Aznif with his sword. Then he picked up her limp body and flung it into a large crater-like hole.

The girls were terror-stricken and did not know what to do. They were well hidden by some heavy bushes and prayed that they would not be discovered by the soldier. If he found them, there would be no chance of survival.

This was a nightmare. Satenig and Yestair huddled together, holding their baby sister between them. Where was God? Why was this happening to their family? She had no idea what to do or where to go. She put her finger to her lips to remind the girls to remain silent and prayed that they would be kept safe and unharmed.

Suddenly, they heard the rumble of thunder and then a loud crack of lightning. It began to rain heavily, which was timely, because the soldier hastily climbed onto his horse and rode away.

The heavenly rain poured down their faces and blended with the tears that were coming from their eyes.

Chapter 7

Aznif in the Pit

AZNIF WOKE UP IN EXCRUCIATING pain. Her left shoulder hurt as though a hot iron was searing her flesh. The agonizing pain made her gasp. She tried to sit up, but she had little strength. After she closed her eyes, Aznif took a deep breath and again tried to lift herself up. When she touched her arm, she felt a sticky wetness on her fingers. Looking down, she was surprised to see that her hand was covered with blood.

Aznif was terrified. Slowly, she began to remember what had happened and she felt her body begin to tremble as she thought about the horror of her parent's death. What would she do without them? How could she live without her beloved family?

She was so saddened by her brother, Aram's death. He was always so full of life and he had so many hopes and dreams when he grew up, and now those dreams were gone forever. Her eyes filled with tears and she began to sob.

Aznif slowly began to remember what had happened when she and her sisters ran away from their house. She recalled that she had been running in the woods with her three sisters when she tripped over a log and fell to the ground. Stunned by the impact of the fall, she must have passed out.

She remembered hearing the sound of a horse galloping toward her. She turned her head and realized that the rider was a Turkish soldier who was shouting obscenities at her and ordering her to stop, but her natural instinct was to run away.

She recalled getting up and running as fast as she was able to go. As she ran, she glanced behind her, and to her horror, she saw a soldier heading toward her. She was frozen with fear. Then she saw him raise a long saber. He slashed her on her left shoulder and arm. Aznif screamed in pain, and her world turned to darkness.

Aznif was disoriented when she finally regained consciousness. She cautiously looked around and realized that she was lying in a large open pit. She wondered where she was. There was a strong metallic smell of blood and the fetid stench of rotting human flesh. When she looked to her right, Aznif saw that she was not alone. She was surrounded by dead people!

She began to wail, "Where am I? Where are my sisters? Why did they leave me?" She thought that perhaps this was just a terrible dream and she would soon wake up and see that everything was fine.

Aznif tried to raise herself up from the foul-smelling pit, but she fell backward from weakness and loss of blood. Again, she attempted to get up but to no avail. Trying to support herself, she placed her hands on either side of her weakened body when she felt something soft.

Aznif looked down to see what it was and screamed when she realized that it was the body of a young boy. His eyes were open, and he seemed to be staring right at her; however, she knew he saw nothing. He was dead.

She cried, "No, no! That's Andrew, my friend from school!"

One side of the boy's skull was smashed in, and his head was covered with blood. Aznif began to shake violently, and then she vomited until there was nothing left in her stomach but some bitter bile. She passed out once again.

When she awoke, Aznif looked around and realized that everyone in the mass grave was dead. She knew that she was also going to die.

She cried out to God.

"Father, I am so weak, and I know that soon I will be with you. Please take me quickly. You know how alone and frightened I am. I want to be with Papa, Mama, and my brother, Aram.

"I will never leave you, nor forsake you."

She knew that her heavenly Father loved her, just as Papa had always told her.

Suddenly Aznif heard a noise.

It was the sound of a woman's gentle voice.

Aznif smiled. "Mama, Mama, is that you? I knew you would find me! I'm hurting so much. Help me, Mama, please," she whimpered.

"Don't be afraid, little one. I have come to help you."

Aznif looked up and saw a woman standing at the edge of the pit. Her head was covered with a scarf, and she spoke in Turkish. When Aznif realized that it was not her mother, her eyes filled with tears, and she began to tremble.

"W-W-Where is my mama?" she wailed.

It was obvious to the woman that the child was delirious and in a great deal of pain.

She calmly spoke to her, "I do not know where your mother is, but don't be frightened. I will help you. Your arm is bleeding, so try not to move."

"Oh, my dear girl, you have vomited all over yourself. Please, don't be afraid. Everything will be all right."

The woman began to climb into the mass grave. She cupped her hand over her nose and mouth because of the malodorous stench from the decaying bodies. She slowly and carefully walked in a stooped position.

Aznif watched as the woman struggled to walk. After several minutes of trying to keep her balance without tripping over the bodies, the woman breathed a sigh of relief when she finally reached the small child.

"I am going to wrap your arm with my scarf to help stop the bleeding," she told the trembling little girl.

She removed her head scarf and carefully wrapped it around Aznif's wound.

The woman's heart went out to the child. She was aware of the atrocities that were occurring throughout Turkey and the thousands of innocent lives that were being lost.

She did not agree with the government's plan and thought that if she could save one innocent child's life, she would do it, even at the risk of losing her own life.

Aznif understood a little Turkish, but she was so confused and frightened that she had difficulty understanding what the woman was trying to tell her. She was extremely apprehensive but she was so thankful for the woman's kindness and concern. She knew she had no other choice but to trust her.

Aznif knew that this was an answer to her prayer. She thanked God for sending someone to rescue her.

The woman tried to lift Aznif up, but it was very difficult to balance herself and the child at the same time. She bent down and very carefully hooked the little girl's good arm around her neck. Then she gently lifted her up.

Aznif was writhing in pain.

"I am so sorry, little one. I know you are in terrible pain, but I must get you out of this dreadful pit as quickly as I can."

Slowly, they inched their way to the edge of the pit. The woman took a deep breath and lifted the child up into her arms and placed her on the ground.

She gently eased Aznif into a small horse-drawn wagon and drove away.

Chapter 8

The Cave

FEARING FOR THEIR LIVES, THE terrified sisters fled farther into the forest for safety. Satenig was struggling as she tried to carry her little sister, Baizar. Yestair was burdened down with their possessions.

When they thought they were out of danger, the exhausted girls decided to stop and catch their breath. They were trembling from shock and were weak from hunger.

Baizar began to cry, "Where are we? I want Mama. I don't like this scary forest! Oh, please, can we go home now?"

Not knowing what to tell the child, the older girls just stared at one another and did not utter a word.

"Where is Aznif?" Baizar asked.

"We have to wait for her. She is all alone, and she must be very scared. I know I would be afraid if I was all alone. You won't leave me, will you?"

No one answered.

"Don't you dare leave me!" I want to go back home! I want my Mama, not you," she screamed. You won't leave me, will you?" she repeated.

Satenig shook her head. "Don't worry, Baizar. You know we will never leave you."

She paused, not knowing what to say to the child. "I really don't know where Aznif is. Maybe we will find her soon."

Baizar began to cry. "I need her! She always takes care of me. She's my very bestest friend! Everybody is gone—Papa, Mama, Aram, and now Aznif. Why, why, why?" she screamed.

"Now you listen to me. Stop your crying and keep quiet! Sit down and don't you dare make another sound," Yestair firmly said.

Satenig picked up her little sister and placed her on her lap. She closed her eyes and began to pray. "Lord, please help us. We are so confused and have no where to go."

Satenig was overwhelmed and felt like the weight of the world was on her shoulders. As a twelve year old girl, she felt so helpless and frightened. She felt very responsible for her younger sisters. She lowered her head and prayed that she would make the right choices for her siblings and herself.

She asked the Lord for help and for wisdom. She didn't want to make a wrong decision that would put her sisters and herself in danger.

Yestair saw the troubled look on Satenig's face and asked her what was wrong. She knew that Satenig was very upset and questioned why the Lord had allowed this to happen to them.

Yestair put her arm around her sister and hugged her tightly. She felt Satenig's shoulders shaking and she gently stroked her sister's hair.

Satenig felt better and in a short while they gathered their belongings and continued on their journey. Miraculously, Baizar had calmed down and held onto her sisters' hands as she walked silently between them.

Darkness was about to claim this horrific day, and the cold night air chilled their tired bodies. The girls continued to walk until they found a secluded spot near some thick bushes. They felt safer near the dense foliage. The exhausted sisters huddled close together for warmth and comfort. Yestair took the blanket that their mother had wrapped around their personal items. The girls wrapped themselves in the cozy blanket and they soon fell into a deep sleep.

They were awakened by the sound of galloping horses. Baizar's eyes flew open, and she was about to speak when Yestair quickly put her finger to her lips and shook her head back and forth. She prayed that her sister would not cry out or make a sound.

Baizar tightened her grip on her sisters' arms, squeezed her eyes shut, and did not make a sound. All three girls were numb with fear. They held their breath until the soldiers rode by.

When Satenig looked around and did not see any sign of the soldiers, she breathed a sigh of relief.

She then whispered, "We have to find a more secluded place. These trees are not safe enough, so let's leave and look around for a better place to hide. I'm sure there are some caves in those mountains up there."

They gathered their possessions and began the long trek toward the huge mountain that loomed above them.

The girls weaved through the dense trees, and soon, they spotted an opening in the side of a mountain that led to a cave. They were elated because they knew that the cave would be a safe refuge for them. Even their frightened little four-year-old sister smiled and seemed to be relieved.

Although they were happy to have found a good hiding place, the sisters were apprehensive about walking into the dark opening. Satenig was terrified to go inside but knew she had no other choice. She stood very still, staring at the ominous-looking cave.

She was having second thoughts about entering the cave when Yestair exclaimed, "Wait a minute!"

Satenig's heart jumped in her chest. "What's the matter?" she asked as she held her hand against her heart.

"Oh, I'm sorry if I frightened you, Satenig, but I just thought of something", Yestair said.

"Do you remember when Papa took us hiking last year? We walked for a long distance until we came to a cave. It had a tall tree near the entrance, just like this one. I think this may be the same cave!"

"I remember asking Papa what was in that big hole."

He just laughed and said, 'Well, let's go inside and investigate. I told him that I didn't want to go in there because it looked dark and scary."

How she wished that their dear father was with them now.

"Just hold my hand, *aghcheekes* (my daughter). I will protect you. There is nothing to fear," he said.

"Then Papa led the way into the cave. We were so surprised to see how roomy and cool it was inside. I remember how Papa directed us to the water dripping from the inner wall. He tasted the water to show us that it was clean. We swiftly drank the refreshing water from his cupped hands."

"So you see, there is nothing to be afraid of. This is a perfect hiding place!" Yestair exclaimed.

"Oh, yes, I do remember that day," Satenig replied.

"Okay, let's go in and take a look around."

More confident, the three girls held hands and cautiously stepped into the dark opening of the cave.

"Do you think there's a mountain lion or a bear hiding in there?" Baizar asked tremulously.

"Don't worry, sweetheart," said Satenig. "We will protect you. Remember, that's what Papa said last year and everything was just fine."

Thankfully, the cave was empty and pleasingly cool. After they looked all around the interior and found nothing to be afraid of, they chose a flat area to sit down. They were exhausted and weary from the trauma of the last twenty-four hours.

Satenig and Yestair spread out their blanket and placed little Baizar between them to comfort their little sister. They thanked the Lord for their safety. Then they wrapped themselves snuggly in the warm blanket and took a much-needed nap.

After a short while, Baizar began to cry.

"My belly hurts, and I am very thirsty," she whined. "I want Mama. I need her," she loudly wailed.

Satenig picked her up and tried to comfort her baby sister, but she cried even louder. She put her hand on Baizar's forehead and realized that she felt feverish. The poor child began to cough and hiccup loudly.

Yestair opened the jug of water and gave her sister a few small sips of water, which seemed to help soothe her throat.

Satenig was worried about her sister's hacking cough. Again, Satenig felt tension in her head and shoulders as she undertook the role of a mother. She was filled with ankst but she tried to act confident in her attitude. She silently prayed that Baizar would soon be feeling better.

Finally, the coughing spasm subsided, and Baizar began to calm down. The poor little one had such a traumatic day. It was understandable that the child was feeling ill.

When Baizar felt a little better and had quieted down, Satenig said, "Everything is all right now. We are safe, and I have something for you, Baizar."

She dug into her sack and took out a piece of cheoreg. When Satenig looked at the biscuit, she gasped, and tears began to pour down her face. The biscuit was in the shape of an "A," and she saw that it was the initial that Aram had "invented" so that no one would eat his cheoreg by mistake.

The pain of seeing her happy, fun loving little brother's "invention" was so powerful that Satenig almost felt physically ill.

Why did an innocent boy have to suffer and die by the sword? she thought. How could this have happened to their family? Was it only yesterday that Aram was so happy and full of life? Now he was gone forever.

Satenig often wondered what would have happened if Aram had not been playing outside when the Turkish soldiers came to their house that terrible day.

If their father hadn't run to his son, perhaps things would have ended differently. She loved them both so much and felt so terribly sad everytime she thought of her beloved family.

Yestair saw Satenig's tears and knew what her sister was thinking since Satenig had verbalized to her sister how she felt about the massacre of the family. She felt angry and began to sob loudly. The three girls held on to one another, trying to get some comfort from one another, but it was to no avail. Each of the sisters was having difficulty dealing with the realization that their lives had changed forever. They were now orphans and on their own.

Baizar gently patted Satenig's arm. "Please don't cry, *kourig* (sister). I promise I'll be a good girl."

Satenig tightly hugged her sweet little sister and forced a smile on her face. Although her heart was breaking, she tried to control her emotions for the sake of her two younger siblings.

The girls soon fell asleep. When they woke up, they saw a beam of sunlight peeking into the cave. There was a sound of water coming from somewhere. Satenig knew that caverns formed natural cisterns when moisture drips down the rough surface of the caves.

They walked further into the cave and saw a stream of water. They cupped their hands, just as their Papa showed them and drank thirstily until they were satisfied. Yestair refilled the almost empty jug with the cool, clean water.

The sisters were reminded of the wonderful memories they had with Papa that day. They thanked God for His provisions.

Chapter 9

Arya

AZNIF WAS STARTLED WHEN SHE woke up. She was disoriented and did not know where she was. She was in a strange house and heard the sound of running water.

As Aznif looked around, she saw a woman who was filling a basin with warm, soapy water. She stared at the heavy woman, and then she slowly began to remember. This was the same Turkish woman who had pulled her out of the foul-smelling mass grave. As she thought of that horrifying experience, Aznif started to whimper, and her eyes welled up with tears.

When the woman heard the moans, she turned and walked toward Aznif, who was so frightened that she covered her face with her hands. She was afraid to look at the woman and was fearful of her intentions.

"Ah, I see that you are awake. How do you feel, little one? Do you remember me?"

Aznif gave a slight nod of her head.

"My name is Arya. What is your name?"

"My name is Aznif Kerbajian.

"My sisters and I were running in the woods, when I fell down. I must have passed out because when I woke up, my sisters were gone."

Arya looked sadly at the little girl, and her heart went out to her.

The small child reminded Arya of her own dear daughter who had tragically died when she was seven years old. Arya's husband had been ill with influenza and their little girl had caught the disease from her father. Within a few weeks, Arya had lost the two people that she had loved most in the world.

When she had driven by and heard a young child crying in the foul-smelling grave, she knew that she had to help the child. Without a second thought, she climbed into the large, body-filled pit and picked up the tiny girl and took her home.

"I'm so sorry, but I do not know where your sisters are. Don't be upset. Everything will be all right. Now please try to relax. I have a basin here with some warm water in it. I'm going to wash your body because you were lying in that filthy ditch. You have some deep gashes on your arm and shoulder. I will need to clean the wounds, and then I'll put some ointment on the cuts."

Arya began to carefully wash the young girl's body with warm water. She gently patted her dry and then dabbed a strong medicine onto the wounds. Aznif screamed and writhed in pain.

"Oh, I'm so sorry, my dear. I know it is tender, but I must do this so you will not get an infection in your arm and shoulder."

Tears poured down Aznif's face, and she held her breath as Arya continued to take care of her deep wounds. Aznif was frightened, but she tried not to cry out from the excruciating pain. Arya could see that the child was having a difficult time trying to remain calm.

"You are such a brave little girl. I know that you will be feeling much better in a short while."

Aznif began to feel a little more relaxed in the warm bath as the woman continued to gently cleanse her body.

As Arya washed Aznif's tear-stained face, she noticed the earrings that the child was wearing.

"I am going to remove your earrings because they are encrusted with dried blood and they need to be cleaned. Is that all right?"

Reluctantly, Aznif nodded her head in agreement.

Arya removed the beautiful earrings, cleaned them, and then placed them into the pocket of her apron.

Aznif cried, "Oh, no, please do not take my earrings. They are so precious to me. They were my mama's earrings. Papa gave them to her on their fifteenth wedding anniversary. I can still remember how carefully Mama took off the paper that the earrings were wrapped in. Even the paper was very special to her because Papa printed her name and had hand-painted beautiful pink roses on the packaging."

"Papa was such a talented artist. He loved to paint cute little animals on the front of our birthday cards. Every year, we all looked forward to receiving our own personalized greeting card."

Aznif began to sob uncontrollably. "Now those earrings are the only thing I have left in my life!"

Arya gently hugged the distressed little child and whispered, "Please try to calm down, Aznif. You mustn't upset yourself. I want you to lie down on the bed and try to sleep for a little while. You will feel better after a nap. Will you do that for me?"

Aznif nodded her head.

Arya led her to a small cot in her bedroom. She carefully put the girl to bed and covered her frail body with a light blanket, and noticed that the child started to relax.

"I'll never forget how excited and happy Mama was when Papa gave her the earrings. She passed them around the kitchen table while we were eating dinner so everyone could see how pretty they were. I asked Mama if I could try them on to see how they looked on me. Mama said I could, but I had to be careful not to drop them."

Aznif wailed, "Shortly after that, they were killed!"

Arya slowly shook her head and hugged the child.

"My parents and my brother were murdered! Then my sisters and I ran away, and now I don't know where they are. All I can remember is falling down and then I was in lots of pain. I guess I must have passed out." Aznif started to wail loudly, and her frail body shook uncontrollably.

Arya looked sadly at the orphaned child. She patted her on the back.

"I am so sorry for you and your family, Aznif. You are here now, and you are safe, and no one will harm you. I know it is difficult but try not to think about what has happened. I will take care of you and I will help you in any way that I can, all right? Now close your eyes, my dear, and try to sleep for a little while. I'll be in the kitchen making us something to eat."

She tucked the blanket around the child. Almost instantly, Aznif closed her eyes and fell into a deep sleep.

When she finally woke up a few hours later, Arya came in carrying a tray with a bowl of soup and a slice of warm, buttered bread. Aznif tried to raise herself up, but she was too weak. Arya placed her hand behind the child's back for support and helped her to sit up. Then she spooned the nourishing broth into Aznif's mouth. She was glad to see that the child ate heartily. When she had finished eating, Arya helped her to lie down again. Aznif grinned, closed her eyes, and instantly, went back to sleep.

Later, when Arya heard Aznif stirring, she quietly opened the door and walked over to the bed. She smiled at the little girl and handed her a small box. Aznif took the box, wondering what was in it.

"What is this? Is it for me?" she asked.

"Open it, sweetheart," Arya said.

When Aznif lifted the cover off the box, she cried for joy. "Oh, thank you so much! I am so happy to have Mama's earrings back."

Arya was glad to see the smile on the child's face. She carefully hooked the earrings into Aznif's ear lobes.

"I have cleaned the earrings as best as I could," Arya said.

"They look so pretty on you. Here, let me get a mirror so you can see how nice you look."

She picked up a hand mirror and held it up to Aznif's face. Arya was so happy to finally see a broad smile on the child's face.

"Are you feeling better?" Arya asked.

Aznif shook her head. "No, my arm and shoulder still hurt very much. I can't bear the pain."

Arya touched the child's forehead and realized that she had a fever.

"Perhaps it would be best if I ask the doctor to come to the house to examine your wound." She feared that the deep cuts were infected and realized that she could not do any more for the child without the advice of a doctor.

"Now you stay in bed while I fetch the doctor, okay?"

Aznif nodded her head, closed her eyes, and tried to go back to sleep.

In a short while, the doctor arrived. He carefully looked at the angry wounds and saw that they were badly infected and that the child had a high fever.

"I'm going to clean your arm and shoulder, and then you'll feel better," he told Aznif.

She began to cry. "No, please don't touch it. My arm hurts so much."

"I will be as gentle as I can," the doctor said, "but I must take care of this problem. Now you show me what a big girl you are and try to relax."

He began to clean the deep wounds and then applied a poultice of moist herbs onto the cuts and wrapped the child's arm with a bandage. Aznif screamed from the terrible pain. She began to feel dizzy as she twisted and moaned loudly, and then she fainted.

The doctor handed Arya some laudanum.

"Give the child a teaspoon of this twice a day. It's a strong sedative, but it will keep her in a very relaxed state. If she seems to be getting worse or you see a red line going up her arm, please come and get me immediately. I hope we can save her arm. Do you understand that she is in a very critical condition? We'll know in a few days if the infection has subsided. If it worsens, we may have to take more drastic steps."

Arya sadly nodded her head and thanked the doctor for coming over so quickly. Arya was so depressed about Aznif's health. She thought about the death of her daughter and worried that Aznif, who was in critical condition, might not survive. Arya wept for the poor little orphan. She wiped her tears and quietly tiptoed into the bedroom and was glad to see that Aznif was sleeping soundly.

A few days later, the doctor returned to change the dressing on Aznif's wounds. He was very pleased to see that her fever had subsided and her shoulder and arm seemed to be improving.

As the weeks went by, Aznif slowly began to feel stronger, and the pain grew more bearable. Her appetite was also improving. Arya cooked with locally grown herbs that had been used for hundreds of years to help people who were ill or infirmed.

As time passed, a strong bond developed between Arya and Aznif. She learned that Arya had been married and had a young daughter, but sadly, her husband and her daughter were deceased.

Arya was sixty-one years old and had lived alone since their death. She confided to Aznif that she had also lost her parents at an early age and she could readily understand the fear and anguish that Aznif was experiencing in her young and traumatized life.

As the months passed and Aznif's wounds healed, Arya slowly began to teach her how to tat. At first, the small child was frustrated, but eventually from Arya's instruction and encouragement, she began to enjoy tatting intricate lace doilies. When Arya showed her how to edge the sleeves and hems of her dresses with the delicate needlework, Aznif was so excited that she began to add the lace trimmings on all of her clothing.

Eventually, Arya and Aznif did everything together. They grew very close and their closeness was healing for both of them. As the years passed, Aznif began to feel a little happier. Although she always missed her wonderful family, she was thankful for this dear woman, who was always helpful and kind to her.

Each day, they would cook, eat their meals, and then clean the dishes. They both looked forward to going outdoors and tending to their vegetable garden. This was one of Aznif's favorite activities. She loved to see the vegetables grow from the tiny seeds that they had planted. They bartered their freshly grown vegetables and eggs with the local merchants in exchange for sugar, flour, and spices.

At night, Arya taught Aznif to spin wool. She was very impressed at how quickly and eagerly the child learned. She was happy to see a calmer and a more contented attitude from the solemn little girl.

One day, as they were preparing the evening meal, Aznif asked Arya, "I am curious. Why did you take me into your home? You knew that I was Armenian and that I was badly injured, and yet you saved my life. Why did you do that?"

"I know it was hard for you, and I will always be grateful for what you did for me. Thank you, dear Arya. I know I don't say that often enough, but I want you to know that you hold a very special place in my heart."

Arya put her arm around her dear little friend.

"That was such a painful and distressing time for you, Aznif. You were an innocent child who should not have suffered such a terrible loss. Sadly, thousands of others have suffered and died because of man's greed and selfishness. It's a tragedy for a young child like you to have lost everything. I often hear your screams at night. I know you have nightmares about your parents' beheading and the death of your brother, and it breaks my heart to know that you are hurting so badly."

"We had such a happy and wonderful family. We shared much laughter and tears together. My brother, Aram, was such a cheerful and fun-loving boy. He was always laughing and joking around. He was so full of life and couldn't wait to grow up. Aram wanted to be an inventor because he was always building odd things."

Aznif laughed and gulped as the tears filled her eyes.

Arya hugged her small friend.

"Aznif, you will find happiness again. Your whole life is still ahead of you, and your faith in your Lord will see you through the bad times."

"You'll be happy once again. Remember my words, dear one."

He brought me up also out of a horrible pit, out of the miry clay, and set my feet upon a rock, and established my goings.

And he hath put a new song in my mouth, even praise unto our God: many shall see it, and fear, and shall trust in the Lord.

Psalm 40:2-3

Chapter 10
Joining the Caravan

AFTER THEY LEFT THE SAFETY of the cave, the sisters began walking along the mountainside. Their food and water supply was almost depleted. Baizar was not feeling well and was very weak from vomiting and the inability to control her bowels. The poor child was suffering both physically and emotionally.

"I want Mama!" Baizar cried. "I don't want to walk anymore. Please leave me here!"

Satenig stopped, bent down, and held her little sister close to her, which seemed to pacify the child. She prayed and pleaded for the Lord's help. She knew that she could never replace or be a true comfort to her sister who was not doing well, physically or emotionally.

Satenig felt the Lord's presence, and a peace came upon her. Now that her earthly father was gone, she knew that she had to depend completely on her heavenly Father for guidance.

After praying, Satenig felt more relaxed. She soon fell asleep while holding her baby sister, Baizar on her lap. They were sleeping soundly when Yestair shook Satenig's arm, waking her up.

Satenig was startled and asked, "What is it? What has happened?"

"Quick! Take a look down below. There is a caravan of people walking by."

They watched in wonderment at the long procession of men, women, and children walking slowly along the road.

Baizar became very excited. She began jumping up and down. "Look. I can see some mommies and their little children. Can we go down and join them? Let's hurry and climb down this nasty mountain before they go away and we're left here all by ourselves."

Yestair whispered to her sister, "Calm down and keep quiet. You will have to listen to us, do you understand? Now sit down and behave yourself, Baizar!"

Satenig and Yestair began discussing the pros and cons of joining the caravan. They saw that there were gendarmes on horseback who were carrying rifles. Although they were frightened, they were relieved to see people nearby, but they had mixed emotions about leaving the safety of the mountain. Since Baizar was still feeling ill and their water and food supply was almost gone, they knew that they had to do something in order to survive.

As she held her head in her hands, Satenig looked at her sisters and said, "I think we should stay up here in the mountains where we are safe and keep the caravan within our sight. If we see that it is safe to go down the mountain and join them, we'll do so, okay?"

Her sisters seemed disappointed, but they slowly nodded their heads. Satenig knew her sisters were not happy with her suggestion but she was worried about their safety.

Satenig noticed the sadness in their eyes. "Listen, we will wait until it begins to get dark, and when the caravan stops for the evening, we'll try to slip into a family group of people. What do you think, Yestair?"

"I think that is a good idea, but we must be extremely careful. I know it will be very risky, but at this point in our lives, we have no other choice," Yestair sadly replied.

Finally, when darkness came, they noticed that the caravan was beginning to slow down. The girls began to carefully make their way down the rugged mountainside. They hid among the many trees and bushes that were along the side of the road, while they kept an eye out as the people began to settle down for the night. They were within hearing range and realized that a group of refugees were eating and talking quietly among themselves.

The girls were so tired and hungry that they had to restrain themselves from joining the caravan. In a short while, they saw no movement from the refugees. The girls assumed that everyone had gone to sleep for the night. They knew that the travelers must have been as exhausted as they were.

When it appeared that everyone was sound asleep, the girls cautiously began to walk toward the back of the caravan. Just as they were about to run toward a wagon, they stopped abruptly. In the darkness, they saw the glow of a cigarette from a gendarme who was standing near the wagon.

Motioning silently, Yestair pointed to the man. They waited patiently until he had finished smoking. He then began to walk toward another guard who was down the road. The two men started talking, and then they began to laugh loudly.

The two gendarmes went to join one of the other guards who was cleaning his equipment for the following day's journey. The three men were busy wiping down their gear and were deep in conversation.

When it seemed safe, the girls ran quickly and slipped into a latge group of refugees. They had to find a place to hide. Satenig spotted a wagon nearby, and the girls crawled under it for safety. When she looked up, Satenig saw that there were long slats of wood on the undercarriage of the wagon. The slats were used to store packages or extra equipment.

She whispered, "I think we're small enough to wedge our bodies into the bottom of the wagon so the gendarmes will not be able to find us. What do you think, Yestair?"

"Yes, that would be a perfect hiding place for us," Yestair agreed. She lifted little Baizar up and placed her on the wooden slats.

"What are you doing? Baizar asked.

"Shh, keep quiet and don't say another word, do you hear me!" Yestair whispered.

Then she and Satenig climbed up and layed down on either side of their little sister in order to comfort the confused and frightened child. They were exhausted and emotionally spent. Although they were uncomfortable under the wagon, they soon feel into a deep sleep.

The next morning, they were awakened by the angry shouts from the guards, ordering the refugees to get ready to move on. The girls awoke, frightened and confused, until they remembered where they were. They remained under the wagon for a long while as the caravan moved deeper into the desert. They were extremely hot and very hungry and thirsty.

The burning sun was high in the sky, and the blowing hot sand made it difficult to breathe. Baizar began to whimper, but her sisters tried to calm her by telling her stories and pretending that this was a great adventure to be hiding under a wagon, where no one could find them. Even though they were very cramped and uncomfortable, they did feel hidden and safe.

Finally, the wagon came to a halt. The sisters did not move, and they remained silent. Then they heard a young girl's voice telling her mother that she wanted to get out of the wagon to stretch her legs. As she began to climb out, the youngster stumbled and fell down. While she was lying on the ground, she looked up and spotted the three girls hiding beneath her family's wagon.

She called, "Mama, come here! There are some girls under our wagon. Who are they?"

Her mother put her finger to her lips, trying to silence her daughter. She knew that if the guards heard a commotion, they would come to investigate, and their lives could be in danger.

She walked to the back of the wagon and saw the terrified girls visibly shaking. She softly asked, "What are you children doing under there?"

Satenig's voice cracked as she said, "We are all alone. Our parents and our brother and sister have been killed. We are so afraid and don't know what to do or where to go."

"Oh, you poor little children, I am so sorry for you. My name is Anahid, and this is my daughter, Mary. You may ride along with us, if you wish."

"We are so sorry—" Yestair mumbled.

"Please . . . there is no need to apologize. I thoroughly understand your predicament. We are happy to be of help. We must support one another during this terrible time. You may ride along with me and my two children. If you see one of the guards coming near us, put your heads down and look busy until they ride away. Never make eye contact with any of the guards. Do you understand?"

The sisters quickly nodded their heads and felt safe for the first time since this terrible ordeal had begun.

Anahid was very kind to the girls. She treated them as though they were part of her family. Even though the food supply was limited, this wonderful woman shared what little she had with the three orphaned children.

The caravan moved continuously forward through the hot desert sand. After they had walked for many hours, the girls grew weary, and some blisters covered the soles of their feet. But they preferred walking rather than lying on their backs on the undercarriage of the wagon.

It was a blessing that the guards never realized that they were there. Thankfully, there were only a dozen or so guards who were watching the hundreds of refugees. They never counted how many people were in the lengthy caravan. All they were concerned with was driving the people deep into the burning desert. They knew that most of them would die from starvation, thirst, or disease. The heartless gendarmes deprived the refugees of water and food and forced them to walk under the burning, hot sun. Many of the elderly men and women died from exhaustion and dehydration.

As each day passed, it became more of a challenge to survive this living nightmare. The cruel guards laughed at and taunted the old and weak refugees.

One day, several guards saw two old men who were walking very slowly. One of the guards rode up to them, pulled out a long whip, and began to strike the men as they screamed, "*Yallah! Yallah!* (Hurry up! Hurry up!)

The elderly men attempted to move faster, but they had little strength. One of the guards kept poking them with a rod, and another guard struck the two men with his rifle, causing them to stumble and fall.

Then one of the gendarmes yelled, "Stand up, you old fools!"

When the men struggled to get up on their shaky legs, one of the guards raced toward them on his horse and bayoneted the weakened old men. Then with the toe of his heavy boot, the guard pushed their lifeless bodies into a ditch and laughed.

"Now they don't have to worry about walking!" he yelled.

When the girls saw that horrific act of cruelty, Baizar began to scream. Satenig immediately put her hand firmly on the child's mouth to muffle her scream. She stared deeply into her sister's eyes and shook her head firmly back and forth. The terrified child immediately fell silent.

The weak and starving refugees suffered daily indignities from the cruel and inhumane treatment of the gendarmes. Their sadistic acts proved to be a very effective way of keeping everyone in constant fear and under control.

Chapter 11

Life in the Desert

WITH EACH PASSING DAY, LIFE in the caravan grew more stressful. Most of the refugees, including the elderly and mothers who were carrying their children, were forced to walk in the burning desert for hours without nourishment. The gendarmes knew that most of the people would eventually perish from starvation due to the lack of food and water.

When the caravan came upon a river or an oasis, the heartless guards would not allow the refugees to go near the water. They rode up on their horses and drank noisily, laughing and talking amongst themselves. When they were thoroughly satiated, they would then lead their horses into the water. The animals would drink for a long time and wade in the water, cooling off their perspiring bodies, while the parched refugees patiently waited for their turn.

The women and children could not bear to be so close to the river and yet not be allowed to have a sip of water. The splashing of the water as the horses frolicked in the river was torturous. Many were literally dying of thirst. They were extremely dehydrated, and their swollen tongues were stuck to the roof of their mouths. The children were sobbing for a drop of water. Some people began to run toward the river, but the guards held up their rifles and warned them to get back in line.

One of the guards yelled, "If anyone goes near the water, he or she will be shot. When we are finished and the horses are no longer thirsty, then you will be allowed to approach the river."

Sadly, the weary refugees were treated worse than the animals.

When some mothers begged for water for their children, the guards only laughed and turned away.

"Go ahead. Walk over to the river and see what happens."

One of the guards taunted them as he held his rifle up and placed his finger on the trigger.

The women sadly turned away. They knew how cruel some of the gendarmes were, and they feared for their lives and for the lives of their children.

The extreme temperatures were taxing on everyone. As they marched in the scorching Syrian Desert, the temperatures during the day would often climb to 110 degrees or higher. When the sun went down, the desert became unbearably cold. The gendarmes deliberately forced the caravan of weak and exhausted refugees to walk up long, winding paths and down the sides of the mountains in order to make it more stressful and difficult for the sick and weak ones. The soldiers knew that most of the elderly and the weak would not survive, and that was part of their diabolical plan.

Only a few families were wealthy enough to own a mule or an oxen-driven wagon. Sadly, several hundreds of people had to walk in the hot, burning sun from dawn to dusk. The boring sameness day after day was exhaustive and depressing.

When it was time to sleep, the three tired sisters would spread the one blanket they owned on the hot sand. When the temperatures dropped during the night, they kept warm by huddling together and sharing one another's body heat.

Most of the mothers carried their babies or young children in their arms. Because of this, the women walked very slowly. When a mother stumbled or lagged behind, she would feel the sting of the guard's whip. The constant wailing of the tired and hungry children annoyed the gendarmes, and they would often order the mothers to keep the children quiet. If a mother could not control her child's crying, the guard would take his long whip and strike not only the mother but also her baby.

One day, a woman was slowly trudging along, carrying her infant when the baby began to cry. The mother tried in vain to quiet the child, but the baby only screamed louder. A gendarme rode up to the frantic mother and ordered her to leave her baby by the side of the road. She refused and pleaded with the guard, to no avail. He grew irate when she did not obey him immediately. He pulled out his sword and plunged the weapon through the baby's body and into the mother's chest.

When the girls saw all the blood pouring out of the two impaled bodies, they screamed, and little Baizar fainted. After they witnessed these cruel acts, the girls were terrified and always tried to blend into a large group of people so they would not be easily spotted by the guards.

Satenig could not get that horrendous scene out of her mind. She was distressed by these merciless acts and felt physically ill. Her stomach was upset and she began to retch. Since there was very little food in her stomach, the only thing that came up was some bitter bile.

That repugnant act of cruelty made her angry as she thought about her dear parents and her brother's horrible death.

The brutality of the guards continued day, after relentless day. Some of these gendarmes had been the most vile and mentally deranged prisoners in the Turkish jails. They were released for the sole purpose of taking the refugees into the desert to torment and torture them.

The girls lived in fear every day. Satenig knew that they had made a huge mistake by joining the caravan. She had no idea that this was a death march. Satenig now realized that at any given moment, they could be the next victims of the sadistic guards. Unfortunately, they had no other choice because she knew that three young children would never have survived all by themselves.

They were frustrated and trapped with no way out of this horrifying situation. The girls were despondent, and each passing day was like a living nightmare. They knew it was important to keep a low profile. Satenig prayed with her sisters as they continued on this life-threatening and perilous journey.

For several days, things were fairly quiet. The weary girls felt the unrelenting sun burning their delicate skin, which began to peel off in large sheets. Yestair tried to cover Baizar's arms and her tiny body with an oversized shirt.

"I don't like this big shirt. I can't walk because it is covering my legs," whined Baizar. She sat down on the hot desert sand, refusing to move.

"You stand up this very minute and start walking!" Yestair commanded.

"No. You're not my mother! You can't tell me what to do!" Baizar cried.

Satenig walked over to her sisters. As she looked harshly at them, with a scowl on her face, she angrily said, "Now listen, both of you, stop this arguing immediately, or the guards will hear you and they will take care of you and you will not be able to argue ever again! Do you understand what I am saying?"

The girls stood still and stared at their older sister. They were very surprised at the anger in Satenig's voice. She was usually a quiet and self-controlled type of person, so they knew that she must be very upset with them.

Baizar walked over and put her small arms around Satenig's waist.

"I'm sorry, sister. I'll be quiet, but you know, Satenig, my feet hurt really badly and I am so tired," she said as she began to weep.

"What's the matter with your feet, little one?" asked Satenig.

Baizar held up her foot. "I don't know, but they hurt a lot."

Satenig removed her sister's shoe and gasped when she saw that her tiny foot was a mass of angry blisters. Baizar winced in pain when her sister touched her sore feet.

Satenig saw that the soles of Baizar's shoes were worn thin, and the hot, burning sand had blistered her sister's delicate skin. She did not know what to do for the child. Then she thought that perhaps their friend Anahid might be able to help them.

Satenig picked up her sister and carried her over to Anahid's wagon. When she showed Baizar's feet to Anahid, she said, "Oh, my dear, you must be in a great deal of pain!"

Baizar nodded her head as tears poured down her sunburned face.

Anahid picked up the child and placed her in the wagon. She put some salve on her feet and then wrapped them in a soft rag.

"You may ride in the wagon with my daughter, Mary, for a while. Would you like that?"

"Oh, yes!" Baizar cried as she gave Anahid a big hug.

Although Anahid had lost her husband and young son only a few weeks earlier and was struggling with her own problems, she had enough compassion to help the girls. Satenig was so thankful that the Lord had led them to Anahid's wagon.

At twelve years of age, Satenig was plagued with the responsibility of taking care of her younger siblings. She was very frightened and as insecure as her sisters were, but she knew that she had to remain strong and trust in the Lord. The girls thanked Anahid and left their happy, smiling sister with their friend.

As they walked along, Yestair and Satenig reminisced about how wonderful and full their lives had been just a few short weeks ago. They spoke of how uncertain and frightening their lives had become. It was like living in a continuous nightmare. They were exhausted and relieved when the caravan finally came to a halt at the end of each the day.

One of the guards announced that those who had tents could set them up. Since the girls did not have a tent, Anahid made a simple covering for the two sisters. She gave them a couple of old sheets and a long piece of wood that she had in her wagon. Together, they constructed a makeshift tent. Satenig and Yestair were thrilled with their little "tent" because they had some privacy when they went to sleep at night.

One day, as the caravan passed through a small village. They were shocked to see four young women who had been crucified. Their nude bodies were nailed to four crudely constructed wooden crosses. They had nails in their hands and feet and their long hair hung down to their chests from their bowed heads.

Terrified by the gruesome scene, the girls looked away, but they could not get that horrible picture out of their minds. Satenig had covered Baizar's eyes with her hand, praying that the little one did not see what had happened to the unfortunate women. All they could do was pray and try to survive through each dreadful day.

Satenig was very discouraged, but she tried to keep her spirits up, not only for herself, but also for her two younger siblings.

She often thought about their life before this nightmare had begun. She had taken everything for granted. Satenig missed her parents and the antics of her happy, full-of-life younger brother. She thought about the family sitting around their warm, cozy toneer, and sharing their thoughts and talking about their day at school.

Those memories encouraged her but also saddened her, knowing that life as she knew it, was a thing of the past.

At times, when the caravan would settle down for the night, nomadic tribes would descend from nearby mountains and terrorize the caravan. The gendarmes allowed the nomads to take whatever they wanted from the poor, defenseless refugees. The men would attack like hawks after their prey. They would steal food, water, clothing, and anything they thought was of value.

The final affront was when the gendarmes attacked the terrified women who cried and screamed as the women were carried away by the nomads.

Sadly, they were never seen again. The gendarmes looked the other way, not caring what the thieves did to the women.

As the long, arduous days passed, everyone grew weaker from the lack of food and water. Some of the people had to resort to mixing grass with the horses' urine to get any kind of nourishment for their emaciated bodies. Many developed dysentery, and some died along the road. The gendarmes would walk over, and with their boots, they would push the dead bodies into a ditch near the side of the road. They would just saunter away, with sardonic smirks on their faces, as though nothing of importance had just occurred.

The daily stress of watching people starving, growing sick and dying, greatly distressed the sisters. They grew quiet and sullen. Their life was becoming more difficult with each passing day.

Chapter 12

Arya Dies

FOR YEARS, AZNIF'S LIFE WAS filled with fear and loneliness. Although Arya was always kind and understanding, she could never fill the void that Aznif felt in her heart. She missed her family and the happiness and security of being with her loved ones. Many times, Arya would be awakened in the middle of the night by the terrified screams from the distressed child.

Aznif would often clutch the small pouch containing her mother's pink tourmaline and diamond earrings and hold it to her heart. She could vividly remember her mother's smiling face as she opened the satin pouch and saw the lovely earrings that Papa had given to her for their fifteenth wedding anniversary. Papa loved her so much and always brought her gifts as an expression of his deep love for her. Mama's earrings were the only link to Aznif's happy childhood, and it comforted her when she looked at them.

Arya kept Aznif involved with daily chores. She knew that if the girl was kept busy, she would not dwell on her past and become despondent. They enjoyed working together in the large vegetable garden that was located behind the house. It was Aznif's responsibility to maintain the garden and to pick the ripened vegetables. She also helped to feed the chickens, clean the chicken coop, and gather the eggs in baskets. They lived primarily off the land.

Arya and Aznif followed a daily routine. Each morning, they sat at a small round table where they ate their breakfast and chatted for a while like two old friends. Aznif enjoyed these quiet moments together. After they had cleaned the kitchen, they would prepare to work outdoors. Arya and Aznif took baskets of fresh vegetables and dozens of eggs to the local market in exchange for staples like sugar, flour, and spices that were needed for their cooking and baking.

The years went by quickly, and Arya and Aznif became very close—almost like a mother and daughter.

Although Aznif was eternally grateful for Arya's kindness and her compassion toward her, Aznif was still upset that her life would never be the same. Aznif missed her family every day of her life. When Arya would notice the young girl's silence and her pensive mood, she would attempt to do something to boost the child's melancholy state. Arya would attempt to keep her occupied by suggesting that they go shopping at the bazaar where she would purchase a small trinket for Aznif.

As Aznif's thirteenth birthday approached, Arya asked her what she wanted for her birthday. Aznif said she would love to have a new dress or a Bible. She knew that Arya was not a Christian, and she was uncertain that she would receive a Bible from her.

However, a few weeks later, Aznif was pleasantly surprised when Arya presented her with a beautiful blue and white dress which was trimmed with a lace collar and cuffs. When Aznif lifted the dress from the package, she was so excited to see that a small Bible was tucked in the box. Aznif ran to Arya and gave her a big hug and a kiss on her cheek. She thanked Arya for her gifts and everything that she had done for her.

"Oh, Arya, this is the Bible that my Papa had given to me for our family Bible studies. I had it tucked away in the pocket of my dress when my sisters and I ran away from the house on that terrible day."

Arya's eyes filled with tears. "There is no need to thank me, my dear. When you said that you wanted a Bible for your birthday, I remembered that I had found your book and had put it away for safe keeping. I had forgotten all about it until you mentioned that you wanted a Bible."

Aznif cried with joy and hugged her friend. She thanked God for answering her prayers.

"You have brought so much joy and happiness to a lonely, old woman like me. Aznif, you are a blessing, and you deserve the very best things in life."

Aznif put her arm around Arya and said, "You're not an old woman. 'Old' is when all your hair is pure white. You have only a little bit of white in your beautiful dark brown hair."

"Why, I never thought of that! Not only are you a sweet person, but you are also a smart young lady," said Arya with a laugh.

The two women worked side by side from dawn to dusk. In the springtime, there was always a lot to do. They planted seeds in the garden and repaired some broken parts of fences that surrounded the chicken coops.

Every evening after dinner, Aznif spent many hours tatting, which was difficult but enjoyable. Arya saw that her nimble fingers were soon producing beautiful lace doilies and scarves. As she grew more skillful, Aznif began tatting a tablecloth for the small round table in the kitchen, which she presented to Arya on her sixty-fifth birthday. Arya was very touched by Aznif's thoughtfulness.

"Thank you, my dear girl. I will treasure this tablecloth forever. It is absolutely beautiful!" Arya said as she admired the intricate needlework.

"I am so fortunate to have someone like you to take care of me," Aznif said.

"If you hadn't found me in that dreadful pit and nursed me back to health, I would not be here today. How can I ever thank *you* for saving my life!"

The two dear friends embraced one another.

Arya and Aznif led a simple and contented life. They both enjoyed their quiet and peaceful existence.

As time passed, Arya began to show signs of failing health. She had to depend on Aznif to bathe and dress her, which Aznif did willingly.

She remembered the many times that Arya had taken care of her when she was suffering from the deep wounds she had gotten from the soldier's sword.

Every morning, Aznif prepared breakfast and brought it to Arya's room. Her most requested meal was Aznif's freshly baked Armenian cheoreg along with her homemade yogurt and a small dish of black olives.

One morning, after she had knocked on Arya's bedroom door, Aznif walked in quietly and noticed that her friend did not look well. She placed the breakfast tray beside her bed and asked, "Are you feeling all right, Arya?"

Aznif helped Arya to sit up by placing two pillows behind her back. Arya gave her a weak smile when Aznif placed the tray on her lap. She dunked her cheoreg into her coffee cup and took a tiny bite.

"Aznif, I don't want to alarm you, but I am not well."

"Arya, we all get sick at times. Do you remember when I had that really bad cough that I couldn't get rid of for weeks? I'm sure you will feel better soon," Aznif said as she patted Arya's hand.

"Aznif, I'm afraid this is a little more serious. The doctor said that my heart is not working as well as it should."

"I don't understand this! You'll be all right. I will do all the chores. All you have to do is rest, and you'll soon feel better. You work too hard, but don't worry. I may be little, but I am strong!" Aznif replied as she lifted her arm and clenched her fist, making a muscle in her bicep.

Arya laughed. "I appreciate all your encouragement. Knowing how much you have suffered, I can see that your faith in God has made you strong both physically and emotionally. You have always said to me when bad things come into our lives and we question why, that it is important to trust that God is in control."

Aznif was surprised and happy that Arya was finally beginning to understand what was written in the Bible. She always tried to explain what the passages meant, and slowly, Arya learned and agreed with some of the teachings. Even though Aznif's faith wavered at times, she was happy when she saw that Arya would quietly sit and listen to the young girl when she read to her from the Bible. Aznif had grown to love this compassionate woman and felt indebted to her for all she had done for an orphaned child.

As she had promised, Aznif, who was now fourteen years of age, began taking over Arya's chores along with her own work. She assumed all of the household responsibilities and also tended to the work in the garden. Even though she worked hard, she never complained about her long, exhausting days. She was glad that she could help Arya in her time of need. Aznif knew the Lord had blessed her with a substitute mother, albeit a Turkish one.

Sadly, Arya seemed to be growing weaker with each passing day. The doctor visited her every few weeks, but there was little he could do for her failing heart.

One morning when Aznif knocked on Arya's door, she did not hear her voice. She opened the door and walked over to her bed. She set the tray of food down on a small nightstand. Aznif leaned over and whispered her name as she touched Arya's hand. It was ice cold. She immediately knew that her dear friend was dead.

Not knowing who to turn to, Aznif ran out of the house to seek the doctor. When Aznif told him about Arya, he immediately grabbed his medical bag, and they raced back to the house. The doctor confirmed that Arya had died sometime during the night and said that he would make arrangements to have her body removed. The distraught girl began to sob. She had lost her dear friend, the woman who had been like a mother to her for almost eight years.

A few days later, a handful of people attended the small funeral. Arya had no family at all, and she had very few friends. Aznif grieved over her loss and walked aimlessly around the quiet house. She wondered what would become of her now that Arya was gone. She was in a state of shock and tried to think about her future. What was she going to do?

She was startled when she heard someone knocking on the door. She cautiously opened the door and saw a man who introduced himself.

"My name is Mr. Emir. I am a representative from the office of the Turkish Housing Authority. Now that Arya is deceased, this house will be turned over to the government."

Confused, Aznif asked, "What do you mean? I do not understand what you are talking about."

"Arya has been behind in her payments on the house and also delinquent with her taxes," explained Mr. Emir.

"The government will have to sell the property in order to pay what is past due on the residence."

Aznif could not believe what Mr. Emir was telling her. She explained to him that she was supported solely by Arya and she had no money and no other place to live.

The man stood quietly, just staring at her as he thought about the girl's dilemma.

"Pack your personal belongings and come with me. We will find a place for you to live," he told her.

Aznif did not trust this man. She turned abruptly and ran down the hallway to get away from him.

The man immediately ran after her and grabbed her by the arm.

"Listen to me, young lady; don't make this more difficult for yourself. Now you pack up your personal belongings, and nothing else, and then follow me!"

Aznif knew she had no recourse. She slowly walked into her room and filled a small suitcase with her clothing and some of her treasured items. She took one last look around at what had been her home for the last eight years and closed the bedroom door behind her.

Mr. Emir waited at the door. He took her suitcase and motioned with his hand for her to follow him. As they walked away from the house, Aznif turned around. With tears streaming down her cheeks, she looked for the last time at the home that had been a haven for her.

They climbed into a wagon and drove into town. Mr. Emir stopped in front of a large stone building and told Aznif that this was to be her new home.

A housekeeper greeted them as they walked into the house. She motioned for Aznif to follow her. She led the nervous girl into a room where a rotund man with a long, dark mustache walked over to her.

He turned to the government worker and spoke to the man in a stern voice, "She is small and very thin, but I think she will do."

Immediately, Aznif had a feeling of dread come upon her. Then a woman came into the room and told Aznif to follow her. Frightened and trembling, Aznif did as she was told.

They walked down a long hallway until they came to a set of double doors. When the woman opened the door, Aznif almost fainted. Inside the room, were about a dozen women and young girls dressed in diaphanous clothing, some of the women were seated on silk cushions on a carpeted floor.

Aznif stared wide-eyed, and in a quivering voice, she asked the woman where she was.

The woman sarcastically laughed and said, "Welcome to your new home. You are now part of a Turkish harem. Now go inside, and the girls will explain all your duties and what will be expected of you."

She laughed and closed the door, leaving the frightened girl in a state of shock.

Chapter 13
The Harem

Aznif was numb with fear. She could not believe that she had been placed in a harem. She quickly learned that most of the women in the house were victims just as she was.

Aznif was upset to see that the women were wearing exotic garments. They were lounging on large cushions made of raw silk with tassels dangling from each corner. The women stared at Aznif, but no one acknowledged or spoke to her. She saw an empty chair in the corner and sat down. Aznif kept her eyes focused on the deeply sculptured oriental carpet beneath her trembling feet.

Aznif had heard about sultans and their harems. She was terrified that she would be subjected to living in this decadent environment. She was in a state of panic. She didn't know anyone and had no one to turn to. For the first time in her life, Aznif wanted to die. She put her head in her hands and wept bitter tears.

An older woman, who was in charge of the harem slave girls, walked over to Aznif and instructed her to come with her. When Aznif did not make a move, she grabbed her arm and forced Aznif to stand up.

She led her into a room with a deep sunken bathtub and was told to disrobe. Aznif stepped into a tub that was filled with oily water which had a sweet flowery aroma. Aznif wanted to ask the woman some questions, but she was so frightened that she remained silent and did as she was told.

After she was bathed and perfumed, she was given a garment that was unlike anything that she had ever seen before. Feeling very uncomfortable in the semi-sheer gown, Aznif reluctantly followed the woman into another smaller room.

A guard approached her with a hot branding iron. Aznif was held down by a guard while the iron was pressed into her forehead. A folded towel had been placed between her lips in order to silence her screams. A dark blue dye was then poured onto her burning forehead. She groaned and lost consciousness from the excruciating pain.

When she awakened, Aznif realized that she was back in the room with the other women. She noticed that they had similar tattoo markings on their face, hands, and knees. One of the girls informed her that she was now "marked as a Muslim slave girl."

Aznif eventually understood that each tattoo signified that a woman had been "sold" into another harem. Every time that happened, she was branded with another blue tattoo on her body. One of the girls whispered that whenever the sultan grew tired or bored with one of his concubines, the slave girl would be sold to another wealthy sultan or caliph.

Later, the woman in charge of the concubines summoned Aznif to follow her. Reluctantly, Aznif did as she was told. She was ushered into an elaborately decorated room that was called the oda, where a stout man reclined on some silk cushions. He stared at Aznif for several minutes as he slowly puffed on his hookah pipe. He then turned his head and motioned to the woman in charge to come and speak to him. He told her that although Aznif was very small and thin, he would include her as part of his harem. The woman smiled broadly, nodded her head to the sultan, and led Aznif out of the room.

Aznif could not believe that women were treated as items to be sold to the highest bidder. This dehumanizing treatment was so humiliating. She was fortunate that the sultan was not entirely pleased with her appearance. She knew that she would not be a "favorite" of his and was glad that she was thin and looked like a young child.

Every day was a living nightmare, and Aznif wished that she would die. She often cried, and the other girls in the harem warned her that she must control her emotions. They said she would suffer from more humility if she caused any trouble.

As the months turned into years, Aznif was "sold" into several other harems. Each time, she had to tolerate having another painful tattoo branded onto her body. She was so ashamed of her "badges of slavery." She learned that the girls would squeeze lemon juice on their dark blue marks, hoping that they would lighten or fade away. But no matter how many times they scrubbed and squeezed lemon juice on the marks, the tattoos remained raised and blue.

Occasionally, the girls would be allowed to shop at an outdoor market. They were required to wear heavy caftans, and they had to cover their head and face with a long scarf whenever they were out in public. Aznif looked forward to these outings. Even though some of the shoppers stared openly at the harem women as they passed by and pointed and whispered behind their hands, Aznif was not bothered by their rudeness. These outings were the only time that she felt relaxed and safe.

Compared to the indignities that she was constantly subjected to, Aznif still felt safer among the many shoppers, even though, they looked down at her and the other women from the harem with disdain.

Two or three palace guards always accompanied the girls. They kept them within their view at all times while the women shopped. Their dark brown eyes were continually shifting back and forth to make sure that no one attempted to escape. If any of the women ran away during their watch, they would be severely punished.

Aznif continued to pray that the Lord would protect her and give her the strength to endure each day. Although she was continually anxious and distressed, she knew in her heart that the Lord was watching over her. He had healed her wounds and sent Arya, who had taken her into her home, nursed her back to health, and been like a mother to her for many years.

Aznif had grown very quiet and withdrawn during this terrible time as she was sold from one harem to another. She was almost seventeen years old, but she felt much older than her years. She kept to herself as much as possible.

When she was finally alone at night, Aznif would read her small Bible that she kept hidden in a leather pouch. She treasured her Bible that Arya had given to her for her birthday. One of her favorite books of the Bible was the Book of Job. It comforted her to read about how Job dealt with his suffering. He stood firm in his beliefs, never wavering during his trials, and the Lord blessed him greatly at the end of his life. The story of Job encouraged Aznif to keep persevering and it helped her to remain strong in her convictions.

One night as she was reading about Esther in the Old Testament, Aznif realized that her life in some ways paralleled Esther's life. Both Aznif and Esther had lost their father and mother at an early age. Esther was raised by her Uncle Mordecai. He brought her to the king's palace and placed her in a harem. The king favored Esther, and soon, she became his queen.

One day, her Uncle Mordecai told Esther that a decree had been issued that all the Jews throughout the land were to be killed. When Esther heard this, she decided to tell the king that she was a Jew.

Her uncle Mordecai was very upset and told Esther if she did that, she might lose her life.

Esther boldly replied, "If I perish, I perish."

The king was surprised when he heard that she was a Jew, but he loved Esther so much that he stopped the decree, which saved the lives of all the Jews who lived throughout the land.

When Aznif finished reading the book of Esther, she understood that she must be bold and do what she felt was the right thing to do. She began to plan a way to escape from the harem. She knew that if she was caught, she would be put to death.

She thought to herself, that if she were caught and ordered to be put to death, then so be it. "If I perish, I perish."

Aznif felt she would rather die than continue living in yet another decadent harem. She knew that she could not continue to live in this immoral lifestyle.

Aznif was fully aware that if she was caught, she would be put to death. Yet she was willing to take that risk, although she was filled with fear and apprehension.

Aznif knew she had a slim chance of being successful with her plan to escape but anything was better than the indignaties that she had to endure every day. She could not continue to live with the thought of returning to that depraved existence.

After she read about Esther, Aznif began to pray that things would change for the better. She prayed fervently and remembered "not to lean on her own understanding but to trust in the Lord always and He would direct her path."

The Lord had brought her through the horrendous massacre of her family, and He had led her out of the foul-smelling mass grave. He sent a kind woman who "just happened" to be passing by and heard Aznif's cry. She had taken the hurt and bleeding child home and cared for her for many years.

Yes, indeed, Aznif knew her heavenly Father was watching over her. It gave her a sense of hope and the strength to continue on.

Living in this accursed land was more than Aznif could bear. Turkey held nothing but deep sorrow and terrible memories for her. She was obsessed with the idea of escaping. She knew that she would rather die than suffer the indignities of her daily life. She continued to pray every day for God to open the door to a better life, a life where she could hold her head up without fear of what the day or night might bring.

Knowing that the Lord had been helping her throughout her ordeal, Aznif suddenly felt uplifted and encouraged for the first time in many years.

Aznif began to make a plan. She prayed that she would have an opportunity to slip away from the harem guards who constantly watched the women while they were shopping at the outdoor bazaar. She planned to hide for a while and then casually walk near a crowd of people.

It was fortunate that Aznif had only one blue mark visible on her face. She always wore her favorite dress under her heavy caftan. Her long-sleeved and ankle-length dress concealed the tattoos on her knees and arms.

Each time they went to the market, Aznif looked for an opportunity to escape. Finally, after a few months, a large group of the harem women started out one afternoon for the big spring opening of a new outdoor market place. The streets were filled with hundreds of shoppers.

One of the women from the harem was sampling a piece of broiled lamb meat when she began to choke. She was gasping for breath, and her face turned bright red. Some of the women gathered around her and pounded her on the back, but to no avail. One of the guards came to see if he could help to dislodge the piece of meat from the woman's throat. While everyone was involved with helping the woman, Aznif quickly slipped away.

She walked for several blocks until she spotted an alcove in an alleyway. Aznif slipped into the empty recess of the alley and quickly took off her caftan, rolled it into a ball, and hid it in a refuse bin. She then walked in the opposite direction from where the women and the guards were standing.

As Aznif straightened out her wrinkled dress, she spotted a family of five people and casually walked toward them. The father and mother were quite tall, and since she was short in stature and had a slim body, she walked in front of them and tried to blend in with their three children. When they reached the end of the market, Aznif wandered off to an area where a stack of empty boxes were stored and ready to be thrown away. She crawled into one of the large boxes and closed the lid over her head. For the first time since Arya's death, she felt free and completely unafraid of whatever she might encounter.

Aznif was in the box for what seemed like hours. She listened carefully, and when she could no longer hear the vendors hawking their wares, she knew that the market was about to close for the day.

Aznif faintly heard the whistle of a train a short distance away. When it grew dark, she peeked out of the box and saw that everyone was gone except for a few merchants. She walked up to a short, heavyset man and asked him where the train station was. He said he was not sure but thought it was only a few miles east as he pointed his finger in that direction. Aznif thanked the man and began to walk eastward.

Chapter 14

Safe Haven

THE WEARY SISTERS CONTINUED WALKING across the burning Der Zor desert. There were decayed corpses scattered all over the terrain. Body limbs and skulls were bleached white from the sun. The girls were visibly shaken by their surroundings.

The pitiful sounds of the dying and the stench from the innocent people who had already died permeated the atmosphere. Every day, the girls lived with a feeling of angst and were in constant fear for their own lives.

Bedouin tribes would wait in the mountains, knowing that another caravan of refugees would be passing through the area. They knew the Armenians were desperately in need of food and water. They sold their stale bread and warm water at exorbitant prices to the distressed travelers.

Since they were in such weak and poor physical condition, the girls gladly paid the inflated prices. Satenig used some of the precious coins that her mother had sewn into the hems of their skirts. As she was removing the coins, an unexpected tear ran down her sunburned cheek. Satenig cried as she thought about all that they had lost. She knew that their lives, as they knew it, would never be the same again.

One day, the girls saw a nomadic tribe of men riding down from a nearby mountain. They were shouting in an unknown language. Satenig motioned to her sisters to hide under a wagon that was a few feet away from them. As they watched from beneath the wagon, they witnessed the horror of the men as they grabbed some women and young girls and threw them onto their horses. The women were crying and begging the gendarmes to help them. Everyone could hear their heart-wrenching screams as they were taken away.

The guards laughed and looked away, ignoring the abductions. A few of the guards felt sorry for the women but knew that they could not do anything about the situation. One of the gendarmes expressed his thoughts to a guard standing next to him. The look on the other gendarme's face was one of apathy. He shook his head slightly, as he put his finger to his lips indicating that his fellow guard should be silent and not openly express his feelings. With a shrug of his shoulder, he turned and walked away from his friend. Although he felt sorry for the unfortunate women, he knew that he and his friend would suffer severe reprimands from their superiors if they got involved with this terrible situation.

Sadly, the women were never seen again.

Yestair told her sister that they had to protect themselves from these marauding tribes. She said that they had to do something, even if it meant that they could possibly be killed. Satenig reluctantly agreed with her sister but she had no idea what to do.

Eventually, they decided to disguise themselves to look like slovenly old women. They mixed some dirt with a little water and covered their hands and faces with the dark mixture. They began to walk like the elderly, with downcast eyes and hunched-back shoulders. The sisters were blessed that they were successful with their disguise, which protected them from the eyes of the evil men.

There was an elderly man named Peter who walked with the girls in the caravan of refugees. He tried to talk with the sisters and knew that they were very frightened. It appeared that they were alone and he assumed that their family was dead. He decided to befriend the girls.

He was very feeble and walked with a limp. He was also alone because his entire family had been murdered while he had been visiting his sister in the southern part of the country. When Peter returned home, he found that his home had been burned to the ground and his family's remains were inside the demolished house.

As the three sisters walked in the Syrian Desert, they often commented on the dromedary camels walking past them in the opposite direction. The girls were captivated as they watched the dromedaries, and they asked many questions about the intriguing animals.

Peter was an educated man and was able to answer most of their questions. He noticed that little Baizar was staring at the large hump on the camel's back. Peter smiled and knew that the little girl had some questions about the odd-looking animal. He explained to her that camels were often called the "the ships of the desert."

"Do you wonder why camels are found in deserts and not horses or oxen that are very strong?", he asked the little one.

She quickly answered, "Maybe because they are so big and fat?"

Peter laughed. "Well, that is true in a way. Do you see that large hump on the animal's back? That hump is all fat, and this allows the camel to survive when there is no food available. They can drink as much as twenty-five gallons of water without stopping."

He further explained, "God, in His infinite wisdom, had given the camel a third eyelid which allowed the animal to see during a sandstorm. Camels can also close their nostrils to keep the hot sand out of their noses, which make them the only animals that can survive in the desert."

The siblings were very attentive to Peter as he shared his knowledge with them, and they listened to his interesting stories. They learned so much from him as they traveled eastward together, and it helped to pass the time as they walked in the desert. They grew to love the sweet old man, and they were comforted by his presence as they traveled with him. He became a father figure to the girls, and they were thankful for his daily encouragement.

As the gendarmes had predicted, many of the starving and dehydrated refugees did not survive crossing the blazing desert.

Their dear friend, Peter, could not walk any longer.

He explained to the girls, "I need to rest for a while. You must continue moving with the caravan, or you could be in trouble with the gendarmes."

"We will stay with you for a short while," Yestair replied.

"No," he said emphatically. "I will try to catch up with you after I get some rest."

Satenig looked at Yestair and nodded her head toward Peter. The girls put their arms around the prostrate man and attempted to lift him up. After several attempts, they realized that they did not have the strength to lift Peter.

One of the gendarmes saw what the girls were trying to do.

"Leave the old man alone and move along," the guard yelled.

Peter lifted his head, forced a smile on his lips and said, "Please do as the officer says. May the Lord be with you, dear children. He loves you and He will always watch over you."

The girls did not want to leave their dear friend by himself, but they obeyed him.

That was the last time they saw Peter.

Sadly, their dear friend died of dehydration. Their hearts were saddened, once again.

Peter had reminded the girls of their wonderful father. Papa was so kind and was always concerned with his children's welfare. The girls felt safe with Peter and now that he was gone, they once again felt the heartbreak of losing someone that they had grown close to and had loved.

One morning when the girls awoke, they heard the gendarmes' loud voices. They watched them packing their belongings and tying their sacks onto their horses. An elderly refugee asked what was happening. He received a curt reply from a guard that they had completed their job and were now going back home. The girls were upset about this new development. How would they survive without food and water? They prayed that the Lord would lead them to the right path. As the small group of refuges walked through the desert, they began to feel more relaxed without the vicious taunting of the guards.

A week later, as they were heading west, they arrived at an oasis at the border of Lebanon, where they were greeted by a small group of people.

A man walked up to the caravan with a big smile on his face.

"*Paree loos. Eench-spesez?*" (Good morning. How are you?)

The three sisters were so happy to know that these friendly people were Armenians.

Smiling back at the gentleman, one of the older women in the caravan answered, "We are fine, and may I ask who you are, sir?"

"We are from the Near East Relief Organization, and we're here to welcome you to Lebanon. My name is John. My friends and I will be escorting you to the refugee center. There are several groups of NER volunteers who come down to the border and wait for the arrival of the refugees. We are so glad to see you and that you are safe."

"We will be taking you to a big refugee camp which is located on the outskirts of Beirut. Now rest a little while, and then we will be on our way," John announced.

"There is an orphanage for the children who have lost their parents, and there are many kind and concerned volunteers who are taking care of them," he continued.

The girls were so happy and relieved to survive those torturous weeks in the Arabian and Syrian deserts that they began to sob. One of the women from the NER came over and put her arms around the emotional sisters.

"We know how you feel, *aghcheekes* (my girls). Dry your tears. You are safe now. I promise you that no one will ever hurt you again. We are so overjoyed that you have safely arrived."

As they walked toward Beirut, the girls were very embarrassed of their ragged and filthy clothing. They held hands and lowered their eyes to the ground as they silently followed the woman into the city.

The sisters were uncertain when they learned that they would be going to an orphanage where there were children who had lost their parents and were in the same situation as they were.

When they arrived at the camp they saw that most of the children were gaunt and so thin that they looked like walking skeletons with large distended stomachs. Some were fortunate enough to have a parent there who could help and comfort their children. The girls had no one to look after them.

Satenig was so happy to have adults at the orphanage that could now take care of her and her two siblings. She was relieved that she did not have to worry every day about her sisters' welfare. It was a true blessing to finally have some help with their care. She was very grateful for the Near East Relief Organization and the Christian missionary volunteers.

She silently thanked the Lord for His love and for watching over them.

Everyone was traumatized by what they had witnessed while they had travelled for several weeks in the caravan. They continually replayed the brutal deaths of their parents and siblings in their minds. Seeing the horrible crucifixions of the four young girls and hearing the ear-piercing screams of the women as they were carried away by the nomadic tribes was a constant reminder of the cruelty of men.

When they finally arrived at the orphanage, several Red Cross volunteers rushed out to greet the girls, who were so relieved and happy to be with such kind and compassionate people. A volunteer came over and put her arms around the tired young girls. They were happy to hear that there were over four hundred children living in the orphanage who were now strong and healthy.

The women took the three emaciated sisters into a large room where there were several bathtubs. They removed their filthy, ragged clothing, which they disposed of in a nearby trash bin, and proceeded to bathe the girls. One of nurses examined their scalps and saw that their hair was infested with lice. After they washed the girls' hair with a strong solution of soap and disinfectant, they dried them off and dressed them in clean terry-cloth robes.

Because their hair had grown down to their waist, one of the nurses said that it was necessary to cut their hair very short. Satenig pleaded, "Please don't do that. I always wear my hair in long braids."

"I'm sorry, dear. I can see that you have lovely brown hair. But it is full of lice, and I also see a lot of white nits that are clinging onto the long shafts of your hair. Unless we cut it short, these lice eggs will soon hatch. Therefore, the only way we can control this infestation, is to keep your hair very short."

"Don't worry, my dear. It will grow back. Hair does have a habit of growing back quickly," the nurse replied with a smile.

Satenig closed her eyes and mumbled, "I guess you're right."

After their haircuts, the volunteers gave each of the girls some clean clothing and a brand new pair of shoes. All of the clothes had been donations from people in the United States. When the Americans read in the newspapers about the plight of the Armenians, their hearts went out to them. Although the United States was in the midst of World War I, they continually shipped food and clothing to the orphanages in the Near East.

After their baths, the girls were led into a large room that was furnished with dozens of long tables and chairs. For the first time in many months, they had the luxury of sitting down at a table where they were served a delicious hot meal and a glass of cold milk.

The sisters were happier than they had been in a very long time. Every day was new and exciting. They had many new friends who were orphans like they were. The missionaries, who came from various churches in America, helped the Red Cross and the Near East Relief volunteers. They held Bible classes that the girls really enjoyed. Since their father had always read to them and taught his children lessons from the Bible every night after dinner, the girls were happy to be able to attend a Bible study once again. They knew the Lord was watching over them, and they were encouraged by that fact.

One morning, as the girls were eating a delicious breakfast of eggs, bacon, and thick slices of buttered toast, one of the volunteers picked up Baizar's plate and began to take it away. Baizar turned and looked at the woman and burst into tears.

"No, no, please don't take my food."

The surprised volunteer said, "Oh, I am so sorry, sweetheart, I thought you had finished eating. Here's your plate. Please take your time and enjoy the rest of your meal, little one."

Baizar hiccupped and whispered, "Thank you, miss."

The volunteer was more upset than the child was. She could not believe that a tiny bit of food left on a plate would cause a small child to cry. She had to remind herself that these children were very fragile because of the awful experiences that they had suffered over the last few weeks. They needed to learn how to trust adults again and slowly adjust to their new environment.

As the weeks went by, the relaxed and happy children looked forward to each new day. The girls were given a few small tasks. They had to take care of their personal hygiene and clean their sleeping area. They also helped set the tables in the lunch room and then cleaned the tables at the end of the meal. Some older girls washed the dishes, while others were taught how to prepare the food.

The younger children were taught how to read and write. Many had lost their parents at a very young age, so they were eager and happy to learn new skills. The children were kept occupied at all times so they would not have time to fret and cry about their lost families.

One day, a Near East Relief volunteer announced that they were planning to take a trip to the city of Beirut. Since there was a limited amount of seats, the children who were interested in joining the group were required to sign up. Each child would receive a coin to purchase a small souvenir of their choice.

The girls were very excited, and they quickly signed up for the first excursion. The following day, a group of twenty-five eager children climbed into a large wagon with four of the Near East Relief volunteers.

When they approached the busy metropolis, the girls looked around in wide-eyed wonder. They had never seen such a big city. They watched as hundreds of people rushed to and fro. They stared at the beautifully dressed women, as they hurried to their various destinations in the large city.

Satenig held hands with Yestair and little Baizar as they walked slowly around the beautiful city of Beirut. The girls were a little apprehensive and weren't sure where to go. One of the NER women saw the girls looking a little confused.

She asked, "Do you want to visit one of the city's outdoor markets?"

Satenig didn't know what that was and asked, "What will we do at an outdoor market?"

The volunteer smiled, "Oh, my dear, you will be able to buy anything you want with the coins you were given, but be careful and spend your money wisely. Would you like me to take you and your sisters to the market? It will be such fun!"

The girls eagerly nodded in agreement, and off they went in the midst of the crowds. Eventually they came upon rows and rows of stands filled with everything imaginable. There were fruits and vegetables, clothing, beautiful handmade rugs, and jewelry. They looked in awe at the shining jewelry made of jade, coral, and gold.

Baizar spotted a vendor who was selling all kinds of candy and ice cream. There were cold fruit drinks in many different flavors. Her eyes were wide with anticipation. They were so excited that they could not decide what they wanted to buy. Satenig and Yestair bought a large cup of vanilla ice cream while Baizar bought some candy with her precious coins.

They could hardly believe the large abundance of food that lined the streets of the outdoor marketplace. After weeks of near starvation and trying to just survive in the scorching desert, this new life was a little intimidating. Satenig often thought of the thousands who had starved to death during the horrific march through the scalding deserts. She was bitter and often felt angry that innocent lives were lost because of man's selfish desires.

She struggled emotionally as these thoughts flooded her heart and mind. She prayed that God would give her *the peace that passes all understanding.*

The girls continued walking until they approached a vendor who was selling all kinds of colorful ribbons and scarves.

"Oh, I want a pink ribbon for my hair. No, wait. I want the yellow ribbon, or maybe I can get both of them," Baizar said hopefully.

"You can only have one ribbon," Yestair said.

Baizar's lower lip trembled, and she looked as though she was going to cry.

"I'll tell you what, Baizar. I will buy three ribbons, one pink, one blue, and one yellow. When we get back to the orphanage, you may have the first pick of the three ribbons in any color that you want. Is that agreeable with you?" Satenig suggested.

Baizar had a big smile on her face. "Oh, yes, maybe we can share and then switch our ribbons. Then we can ALL have three different colors."

Her sisters smiled at her cleverness and nodded their heads in agreement.

Baizar clapped her hands and said happily, "Oh, I can't wait to get back home!"

The girls walked around the busy market and watched in awe at all the activity and the large amounts of food that were available. Some men were pushing their overflowing carts and calling out their wares. Women were bargaining for better prices, and the haggling was loud and animated. The girls loved the exchanges between the vendors and the shoppers.

Finally, after a long, exciting day, the children were told that it was time to get back into the wagon and return to the orphanage. The volunteers rounded up the tired but happy children, and they laughed and shared their stories about what they had seen and what they had purchased at the outdoor market.

While they were driven home, Yestair picked up a pomegranate that she had bought from a vegetable vendor. She began to remember how much Mama had loved the fruit.

"Do you remember when our brother, Aram, had a piece of sliced pomegranate between his front teeth and bit down on the fruit, making the red juices drip down his chin? Then he ran in and told poor Mama that he had fallen down and had knocked out his teeth. Wow, Papa was so mad at him because he had frightened and upset Mama!"

As the girls remembered the incident, they began to laugh, and then tears rolled down Satenig's cheeks as she thought of her little brother and his mischievous antics. It seemed like a lifetime ago when they didn't have a care in the world and everything was absolutely wonderful. Now it was all gone, and all they had were sad memories.

When they returned to the orphanage, Baizar felt weak. It had been a long, busy day, and Satenig knew that her baby sister had a chronic cough that often flared up whenever she was overly tired. Baizar had developed the cough at the time when they were hiding in the damp cave before they had joined the caravan. The hot desert sun had helped her, but the long, tiring days of walking with little nourishment did not improve her condition. With no doctors or medicine available, the sick child had to endure her bouts of coughing as well as she could. It had been a blessing when their friend, Anahid, allowed Baizar to ride in her wagon whenever she saw that the child was very weak and could not take another step.

Satenig saw that her little sister's eyes were glassy and her complexion had a sallow hue. She took her sister to the nurse in the medical building. The nurse called in the doctor, and after a thorough examination, he saw that her chronic cough had returned and that she had a slight temperature. He gave Baizar some medicine and told the nurse to keep her overnight in the children's ward. The doctor explained to Satenig that her sister had a slight infection in her lungs and she would have to remain in the children's ward until her lungs cleared up.

After a good night's sleep, Baizar was feeling much better, and she asked the doctor if she could go back to her building to stay with her sisters.

The doctor checked her vital signs, smiled, and said, "Yes, you can go, but you must take your medicine every four hours. Will you promise to do that, Baizar?"

"Oh, yes, doctor, I promise". I'll give the medicine to my sister, Satenig. She is very good. She's like my mommy, and she knows how to take care of me."

Baizar was so happy to be back with her sisters and resting in her own little cot, that she obediently took the bitter medicine without any complaints. Within a few weeks, she was back to her normal self. She was happy, and her cheeks were pink and had a healthy glow. Satenig and Yestair thanked the Lord for healing their precious little sister and for protecting and watching over them each day.

A few months later, one of the teachers at the orphanage announced that they would be going on another trip to see the beautiful sandy beaches in Beirut that were situated on the Mediterranean Sea. They were told that they would be given bathing outfits so they could swim in the sparkling blue waters of the sea.

The sisters were a little hesitant. They had never been to a beach that was surrounded by such a huge body of water, and the girls did not know how to swim. A Christian missionary volunteer assured them that there was nothing to fear. She told the girls that there would be several women from the orphanage who would be right next to them if they wished to go into the water.

When they arrived at the beach, the wide-eyed sisters were amazed at the expanse of the enormous sea. Although they had never seen anything so massive and beautiful, they stared at the large span of water with suspicion.

The sisters held hands and began to run toward the water. A young missionary woman spotted the girls nearing the water and ran after them.

"Wait for me! You are not used to this water. Let's hold hands, and we will walk in together," the young woman said.

She knew that the girls did not have any idea of the water's powerful waves and how dangerous it could be.

The excited girls held one another as they reached the water. They were afraid of the waves from the pounding sea, yet they loved the feel of the cold salty water on their legs as they waded cautiously into the ocean. The volunteer stayed with the sisters while they enjoyed the beauty of the Mediterranean Sea.

It had been a fascinating experience, and the girls couldn't wait to return to the orphanage and tell everyone about the fun they had had while they had been "swimming" in the great Mediterranean Sea.

A few months later, their school teacher announced that a class trip to Cairo, the capital of Egypt, was planned for the orphans. She explained that they would be visiting the shrines in Giza, a suburb of Cairo where the pyramids and the Sphinx were located near the Nile River.

Everyone was excited about the trip. Their teacher had described the pyramids, but the children were surprised when they rode up in the horse-drawn wagon. The Great Pyramid was enormous. A guide told the children that the pyramid had been built 4,500 years ago for a rich king who was buried in the tomb. He explained that each of the two million stones had been cut by hand. The height of the pyramid was 481 feet and, it was 750 feet in length. When the girls stood next to the tomb, they felt like a small pebble next to a mountain.

There were two smaller pyramids on each side of the Great Pyramid, which were the tombs for the king's two sons. The group of children walked a short distance, and then they saw the Sphinx. This huge statue looked like a lion with the face of a man. It was seventy-two feet high and one hundred and sixty-four feet long. The Sphinx appeared to be "guarding" the pyramids.

It was a fascinating trip, and everyone was sorry to leave one of the "seven wonders of the world."

When the children returned to the orphanage, they talked endlessly about their experience in Egypt.

Chapter 15

The Train

AZNIF SUCCESSFULLY ESCAPED FROM THE harem guards. She left with the clothes on her back and a small bag containing a change of clothing and a few personal items that she had tied under her long dress.

She had sewn her most precious possession into the seam of her dress—the pair of pink tourmaline and diamond earrings that her father had given to her mother for their fifteenth wedding anniversary.

Aznif kept the earrings well hidden for years after the massacre. When she looked at them, it brought back both good and bad memories. It was shortly after her parent's anniversary that their lives had changed forever.

After she walked for nearly an hour, Aznif noticed some puffs of black smoke curling in the air. She walked toward the smoke until she saw some railroad tracks a short distance away. She was very excited, knowing that she could soon be on a train and away from this accursed land.

Walking as fast as she could, Aznif soon spotted the railroad station. She walked toward the depot and went inside to see the stationmaster, who was standing behind the counter. Aznif was so happy to see someone who might be able to help her.

"Excuse me, sir. Can you tell me when the next train will arrive?"

"Where do you want to go, miss?"

"Well, I have a problem, sir. I have very little money, and I was wondering if you know of anyone that needs the services of a maid. I am a very hard worker, and I will gladly work for the price of a train ticket."

"Listen, young lady, this is not an employment agency! I don't know anyone, and I would appreciate your leaving the station house unless you are going to purchase a train ticket. Now excuse me."

And with that, he abruptly turned his back and walked away.

Aznif went outside and saw that it had turned dark. She spotted a bench near the depot and sat down to rest for a while.

She heard some passengers talking and decided to approach an elderly woman who was about to go into the ticket office. Taking a deep breath, Aznif walked up to the woman.

"Madam, I am short on funds and need some money to purchase a train ticket. Would you be able to help me? I would be happy to work for you in return for your kindness."

The woman looked at her scornfully and replied, "I don't know who you are and I do NOT need any help from you or anyone else. Now get out of my way! I am in a hurry and I need to buy my train ticket."

Aznif slowly walked away and sat down on a bench at the far end of the train station. She tried to hold back her tears.

"How will I ever get away from this area?" she thought to herself.

Aznif pleaded to the Lord to help her once again. She hung her head and closed her eyes.

She was abruptly awakened by the sound of a loud train whistle. Aznif rubbed the sleep from her eyes and looked around. She saw quite a few people waiting to board the train. She noticed a well-dressed woman who was trying to manage her three young children while she struggled with her baggage. Aznif heard her reprimanding her children in Armenian.

Gathering up some courage, Aznif walked up to the woman. "Excuse me, madam. I was wondering if I could be of any help to you.

I know how difficult it is to manage three children while travelling. I heard you speaking to your children in Armenian."

"I am also Armenian. I am very low on funds, and I would gladly take care of your little ones in exchange for a train ticket."

The woman studied the small girl for a moment and then replied, "I could certainly use a little help with the children and my luggage."

Aznif could not believe her good fortune. She silently thanked the Lord for His help.

"You stay here and watch my children while I go inside and buy the tickets. We are going to Beirut. Where are you going?"

Aznif smiled and said, "Oh, I am also going to Beirut!"

She did not know too much about Beirut, but she had no alternative but to go wherever this woman was going.

"My name is Miriam. My children and I are going to Beirut to spend a month with my sister. She is taking care of our elderly mother, who is very ill."

"I love Beirut. It is such a beautiful city, isn't it?

"Well, I really have never been there, but I have heard that it is a lovely city. My name is Aznif Kerbajian, and I am looking for a job. I thought perhaps there would be more job opportunities in a big city like Beirut."

Miriam smiled in agreement. "Oh, yes, there are many jobs available. I'm sure you will not have any problem finding a suitable position."

"Now if you will watch my children for a few minutes, I will go inside and purchase the train tickets."

Aznif could not believe her good fortune.

The conductor called for everyone to board the train. Aznif picked up Miriam's luggage, and they quickly found some empty seats and settled down for the long train ride.

In a short while, the children fell asleep. Aznif asked Miriam what Lebanon was like.

"Well, it is one of the smallest countries in Asia, and it borders Syria and Israel. Beirut is the capital of Lebanon, and it is located near the

Mediterranean Sea. People come from all over because of the white, sandy beaches and the beauty and tranquility of the sea," Miriam replied.

"I sure hope that I can find work there," Aznif said.

"I am seventeen years old and I'm all alone. My entire family was killed during the Armenian massacre in 1915. I had a wonderful family that I miss every day of my life. My father was a teacher and also worked in the Armenian churches, painting murals and sculpting stone figures into the walls of the ancient cathedrals. Mama took care of my three sisters, my brother, and of course, me. They are all gone now." A lone tear rolled down her cheek.

Miriam clasped Aznif's hand and held it tightly. "I am so sorry for your loss." She did not know how to console the sad young woman. "Aznif, you are welcome to stay with me at my sister's house until you can find some kind of work."

Aznif was overjoyed and very thankful for this kind woman's help and concern.

A few hours later, Rashid, Miriam's eldest daughter, awoke. "Mama, look at all those beautiful birds!"

As they glanced out of the train's window, they saw that it was dawn and noticed a flock of golden eagles perched on the majestic trees.

Miriam explained that birds were plentiful in Lebanon because the coastline was an important resting place for the birds as they flew between Africa and Europe.

"What kind of trees are they?" she asked Miriam.

"Lebanon is famous for its cedar trees. As a matter of fact, the cedar tree is the symbol that adorns the Lebanese flag. If you are familiar with the Bible, you may remember that King Solomon built his palace from the wood of the cedar tree."

Aznif's eyes lit up. "That is so interesting. I remember my Papa reading stories to us from the Bible about King Solomon, but I never knew what a cedar tree was or where they grew."

Aznif was very impressed by the beauty of this lovely area and the blue Mediterranean Sea.

The two women talked for quite a long time while they kept their eyes on the youngsters. Aznif offered to play some games with the restless children, and Miriam was very grateful for her help. Knowing that her children were in good hands, she leaned back in her seat, closed her eyes, and rested for a little while.

An hour or so later, the conductor announced, "The next stop is Beirut. We will be arriving at the train station in approximately fifteen minutes. Please start to gather your possessions and check under your seats to be sure that you do not leave anything behind. Thank you and enjoy your stay in this beautiful city."

Aznif looked out of the window, and the sight was breathtaking. The train was running parallel with the Mediterranean Sea and the sun was shining on the sparkling blue water. She was fascinated by the beauty and expanse of the sea. She thought to herself that this was a moment in her life that she would always fondly remember.

She was finally free, and the Lord miraculously had watched over her. Aznif closed her eyes and was thankful to God for bringing Miram and her children into her life.

The train made a turn and began to slow down. Aznif saw crowds of people walking in the busy streets of downtown Beirut. Her heart leapt with joy. She could not believe that she was out of the country of Turkey forever. She knew she would never return there again.

Miriam and Aznif picked up the suitcases and held the children's hands as they waited to disembark. The train slowed to a stop, and they edged their way down the aisle.

When they stepped off the train onto the platform, Aznif felt her stomach tighten. She was a very apprehensive because she did not know what to do next. She glanced at Miriam, who gave her a big smile and motioned with a wave of her hand to follow her.

They were greeted by Miriam's sister, Margaret, and her two young children.

Miriam hugged her sister and the children, and the two women laughed and kissed one another.

"Margaret, I want to introduce you to my travelling companion. Her name is Aznif Kerbajian, and she has been a tremendous help to me on the train. I do not know how I could have managed without her."

Aznif gave her a shy smile as she tried to adjust her wrinkled cotton dress and her tangled hair.

Margaret realized that the poor girl was embarrassed by her clothing and her appearance.

She immediately walked over and gave Aznif a big hug. "Welcome to Beirut. Is this your first visit to our beautiful city?"

Aznif nodded her head. "Yes, it is. I never knew it was such a big city. I feel a little overwhelmed by the crowds of people. I have always lived in a small village and I guess I will have to adjust to all this activity," she said with a smile.

Miriam put her arm around Aznif. "She is looking for a job and doesn't know anyone here. I have invited her to stay with us until she becomes familiar with the area. Is that all right, *Kourig* (sister)?"

"Of course it is. We have an extra bedroom." She turned to Aznif with a smile and said, you're welcome to stay with us," Margaret said warmly.

"Oh, thank you so much! You are both so nice, and I really do appreciate this. But please, I want to be of some help to you both in exchange for your hospitality. I am so very grateful for your kindness," Aznif replied.

"We would be delighted to have your help. I don't know if my sister has explained to you about our mother's debilitating illness. She is bedridden and requires constant care, so we could use all the help we can get. Now come along. Everyone must be tired from that long, musty train ride," Margaret said with a broad smile.

When they arrived at Margaret's house, Aznif was happy to see that it was a very large home with a backyard that was completely fenced in on all four sides. She thought that it would be perfect for the children.

She was already planning various games for the children to play in the beautiful, flower-filled yard.

The house was not far from the ocean, so Aznif hoped to take them to the beach. This would allow Miriam and Margaret some time alone to care for their mother without worrying about the needs of the children.

When Margaret saw how efficient and helpful Aznif was, she knew that she and her sister had made the right decision to bring the young woman into their home. Everyone got along so well.

The children loved Aznif and her kind and gentle ways. Although she was a single young woman, Aznif knew that children enjoyed being with somebody who took the time to play with them.

Every day, they looked forward to "story time," when Aznif read interesting books to the five active children. Aznif enjoyed being with the children, almost as much as the children did. It brought back such wonderful memories of how Papa read stories from the Bible every night to her and her siblings.

The following month, Miriam told Aznif that she and her sister had decided that if Aznif wished to stay with Margaret and her family, she would have free room and board, and she would also receive a small salary. Miriam said that she and the children would be going home the following day.

Aznif hugged her new friend and said, "Oh, I will miss you and the children so much! How can I ever thank you for your kindness, Miriam? I had been worrying about where I would live, and this truly is an answer to my prayers. I thank you and Margaret from the bottom of my heart."

Again, she hugged her friends tightly as her eyes welled up with tears.

"Don't be upset, dear girl. The children and I will also miss you. But we will be returning in a few months to spend the Christmas holiday with the family. We are so glad that you are happy and content here in Beirut.

"Margaret can now relax a little, knowing that she has you to help take care of our mother and her children. Margaret's two little girls are so happy that you will be living here with them. God bless you, Aznif. You, my dear, are an answer to our prayers!"

Early the next morning, Miriam and her three adorable children left for home. Aznif sadly waved good-bye and could not wait for their return at Christmas time.

Chapter 16

Steerage

A SHORT TIME AFTER THE SISTERS returned from their wonderful adventure to the beach on the Mediterranean Sea, Satenig was told to go to the administration office to speak with Miss Wright. She wondered what was wrong and was feeling uneasy as she entered the building. She was concerned about the welfare of her siblings and hoped that there weren't any problems.

Miss Cooper, a representative from the Near East Relief Organization in New York, was in the room with Miss Wright. The two women smiled and warmly greeted Satenig.

Miss Wright told her that she had just received some good news that they had all been anxiously waiting for. She told Satenig that a steamship leaving for the United States would be arriving within the next few weeks.

"We have contacted your aunt and uncle and they are very excited to have you live with them in New York City. They will be waiting for you when the ship arrives in New York harbor," Miss Cooper explained.

Satenig looked at the women with fear and apprehension. Her mind was racing as she thought about what it would be like to leave the orphanage. The idea of a new home frightened her.

Satenig wondered what it would be like to become a child once again. How would it feel to have someone else responsible for the welfare of her sisters?

The sisters were beginning to feel very safe and content since their arrival at the orphanage. It had taken more than two years for them to adjust to their new living conditions. Now the thought of leaving the orphanage was a little frightening.

Satenig took a deep breath and firmly asked, "What about my sisters, Yestir and Baizar? You did not mention them. I could never leave the orphanage without them."

"Oh, of course they will go with you, my dear. We would never separate the three of you. Don't worry about anything, Satenig. Everything will work out just fine."

"Now let me explain the procedure. We need to fill out many forms. You and your sisters must have a complete physical by the doctor. If everything is in order, the three of you will be placed on the passenger list."

Satenig was so relieved to hear that her sisters would be with her. She was more relaxed and was willing to answer the questions that Miss Wright and Miss Cooper required of her.

They filled out many forms concerning each girl's vital statistics. Satenig became very emotional as she provided the names and birthdates of her parents.

Miss Wright nodded her head and said, "We will submit these papers to the people who are in charge of the departure date. When they contact us, we will give you plenty of time for you and your two sisters to prepare for the long journey. You did very well, dear. Now go and tell your sisters the good news."

Satenig thanked both women and ran outside to find her sisters. Yestair and Baizar were playing in the yard behind the orphanage.

"I have some very good news. We will be leaving in a few weeks for America and we'll be living with our aunt and uncle in New York City."

"Isn't that wonderful news?"

Tears were flowing from their eyes. Satenig was surprised to see their reaction.

"Why are you crying? I thought you would be happy since we have been waiting for nearly two years to leave the orphanage. Miss Wright said that since the Great War has ended, it is now safe to travel across the sea once again. Just think, we'll have a wonderful new life, and we'll have many new friends."

"But I have so many friends here, and I don't want to leave them!" Baizar sobbed.

"Well, think about all the new friends you will have in America. Can you imagine what it will be like to live in a wonderful country where there is plenty to eat and many stores in which to shop? We are so fortunate to have an aunt and uncle in the United States who are willing to take care of us."

The girls dried their tears when they realized how truly blessed they were. A smile appeared on Yestair's face.

Three weeks later, the ship finally arrived. The NER volunteers helped to organize and pack the girls' meager possessions, which were then loaded onto a wagon. Twenty-seven other orphans would be sailing with the Kerbajian sisters to the United States.

Everyone left the orphanage with mixed emotions. The girls were happy that they would be living in another country, and yet they were sad that they would be leaving behind all of the people whom they had depended on and had grown to love during the last two years.

The Near East Relief volunteers, the Christian missionaries, and the entire staff of the orphanage hugged and spoke to each of the anxious orphans. They offered words of encouragement and handed each child a small bag of items that they could use on the long ocean voyage. In each bag was a bar of soap, a small washcloth, and other sundry items. The children were excited when they noticed that there were also some cookies and candy in the bottom of the bag.

Finally, it was time to leave. Some of the children had sad faces and were visibly upset. As they climbed aboard the large open wagons, they waved and threw kisses to the wonderful men and women who had taken care of them for more than two years.

When the children saw the enormous steamship in the harbor, they could not wait to climb aboard the huge vessel. Hundreds of people were ascending the gangplank. Eventually, after the first-class and the second-class passengers were aboard the ship, people in the steerage class, which included the small group of children from the orphanage, walked up the gangplank with much anticipation.

When they reached the top deck, they were met by one of the ship's officer, who was dressed in a crisp white uniform and wore a white cap trimmed with gold braid.

He loudly bellowed, "You people, follow this man, and he will show you to your quarters."

The steward led them to a door near the rear of the ship. He motioned with a wave of his hand and said, "Follow me and walk quickly. Now go down this staircase and turn to the left. You will see a large room, which is where you will be staying for the duration of the trip."

Everyone walked carefully down the dark, narrow staircase that led to the room. As they entered, the passengers were assaulted with a strong smell. The awful stench of body odor combined with the heat from the engines was intolerable. This area was in between the top deck and the bottom of the ship, where the engines were located. The room was lined with two tiers of wooden planks around its perimeter, which served as their beds.

The steward tossed a small pillow and a blanket to each of the passengers. Yestair grabbed hold of her blanket and pressed it tightly against her body. As she did this, dozens of cockroaches fell out. The children screamed as the bugs scurried around their feet. When the other children were given their bed coverings, more of the offensive roaches fell onto the floor, and pandemonium broke out in the room.

The angry steward yelled, "Keep quiet, all of you! Just step on the bugs and get used to it because they are everywhere. They are harmless. Just be careful of the rats. Now *they* are nasty!" he said, laughing sarcastically.

"It is so hot down here. These are deplorable conditions!" a male passenger complained.

"This is steerage, and we have close to one hundred passengers down here. If you are not happy with these 'conditions,' then I suggest that you leave right now before the ship sails," the officer snapped. He then abruptly turned around and stomped up the stairs.

It was obvious to everyone that they had no alternative but to try to make the best of the terrible accommodations. The cost to travel steerage was the least expensive way to travel on a steamship. Each passenger paid between fifteen and thirty-five dollars, depending upon his or her age. This included food that was poorly prepared and sometimes inedible.

Members of the crew came downstairs with buckets of food that they doled out in meager proportions. The adult passengers were given watered-down coffee, and the children were served milk, which was often warm and had a sour taste. The hard biscuits had moldy spots on the crust. If the meal was hot and edible, the passengers did not complain. They knew if they were too vocal about the quantity and quality of the food, the servers would report the complaints to the head steward, and then they would be given even smaller portions of the tasteless food.

The passengers were required to wash their own plates and utensils. There were a few small sinks in the dingy bathrooms, which only had lukewarm water. Everyone had to stand in line to wash their plates. The children were impatient and would often whine and misbehave in the cramped and overcrowded rooms.

At times, some of the upper-class passengers would open the door and throw down a few coins or some candy. They enjoyed watching as the people in steerage pushed and shoved one another for a single treasured coin or a tiny gumdrop. The upper-class passengers seemed to enjoy this diversion as they laughed and walked away.

After a few days, some of the children began to get sick to their stomachs and vomited, which made life in the windowless room even more unbearable. The constant noise from the engines below them and the rocking of the boat made many of the children and some of the adult passengers seasick. They needed fresh air, but the steerage passengers were not allowed to go upstairs to the open deck except for one hour each day, which enabled them to breathe in some fresh air from the ocean breezes for a short while.

There were more than thirty people in each of the three large rooms in steerage. A heavy tarp ran down the center of the room, separating the men from the women and children, which provided some privacy to each of the groups.

The men were often helpful and offered some encouragement to the frightened orphans. They lifted their heavy bundles and assisted the younger children when they had to climb up to their bunk beds. Many of the mothers also helped to take care of the younger children's needs. When the orphans were seasick, the adults cleaned up after them and they helped to soothe and comfort the little ones when they were frightened.

In order to pass the time away, the passengers played games. The men enjoyed playing Scambeel, an ancient game of cards that was played in the "old country." They shared stories of their past family lives and talked about what they wanted to do when they reached America.

The men had heard that there were many opportunities available to those who were willing to work hard. They often talked about the stories they had heard of America, where there was freedom for all and where one could live without fear.

During the evening, the children looked forward to hearing the men sing. They would clap their hands and stomp their feet. The men would often sing familiar Armenian folk songs. At times, the women and children would join in the singing.

In the group, there was a young man named Paul who had a talent for making music with his hands. He would moisten his fingers with his tongue and then interlock his hands. With his two extended index fingers, he would create a loud clicking noise that sounded like a rhythmic instrument. He often led the children in traditional folksongs, and the cheerful group would join in the singing and dancing.

Everyone would link their pinkie fingers together and form circles as they danced around and around until they grew tired. After an hour or two of this merriment, the children and the adults were happy and relaxed. They would then go to sleep and enjoy a good night's rest.

Early one morning, the children heard three blasts from the ship's horn, which woke everyone up. Then they heard people yelling and shouting from the deck above. "America! America! We have finally arrived in the United States!"

It seemed like it had taken months to cross the sea, but in reality, it had been only a little more than two weeks since they had begun the long and difficult journey to America.

One of the members of the crew opened the door from the upper deck and called down to the passengers, "We have arrived in New York harbor. You may come up on the deck."

Everyone began to run up the stairs. People were openly crying and hugging one another as they gazed at the tall, magnificent Statue of Liberty standing with her right arm holding a lighted torch.

A crewman read aloud the touching sonnet written by Emma Lazarus, which was engraved on the base of the statue: "Give me your tired, your poor, your huddled masses yearning to be free, the wretched refuse of your teeming shore. Send these, the homeless, tempest-tossed to me. I lift my lamp beside the golden door!"

The awestruck sisters shed tears of happiness as he read the heart-wrenching words and talked about freedom and what it stood for. While they stared at Lady Liberty, the girls grew very excited as they realized that this was to be their new home.

Baizar's eyes were filled with tears.

"I'm so afraid. Do you think we will be all right? I want my Mama and Papa! I don't want to leave this ship. I'm scared!"

Satenig was also feeling very uneasy but she knew how important it was to be brave, not only for her sisters, but also for herself. She had so many questions about all the changes that were about to occur in their lives but she kept her fears to herself.

She embraced her little sister. “Please don’t be afraid. We will all be together and the Lord will be with us. You know how much He loves you and He will always take care of you.”

Satenig knew that they would never be able to return to their homeland and they would be facing many different challenges in this new country.

As the ship continued to head toward the harbor, everyone on board stared at the beautiful city of New York.

“I have never seen so many tall buildings! How do the people get up to the top floors?” Yestair asked.

One of the male passengers overheard the girls talking.

“I was told that some of the buildings are several hundred feet high and they have a box called an ‘elevator’ that you can walk into and ride all the way up to the top of the building. Can you imagine that! Those buildings are so tall that the American Indians had to come and help to build most of these skyscrapers since they are so sure-footed and are not afraid of heights,” he said in amazement.

The sisters listened closely and were fascinated by the information.

Satenig smiled. “See, didn’t I tell you girls that we would have a brand new life. That’s why they call America ‘the land of the free!’

Finally, reality had set in. This was now their new home and they knew they could never go “back home” again.

The three sisters held hands and wept as they gazed at the breathtaking skyline of New York City.

Chapter 17
Ellis Island

EVERYONE HAD GATHERED THEIR POSSESSIONS and waited on the upper deck of the ship. They were fascinated as they watched the huge steamship slowly inch its way into New York Harbor. It had been a long, arduous journey, and the Kerbajian sisters could hardly wait for the boat to reach the dock, which was slowly coming into view.

As the large ocean vessel approached the harbor, they heard and felt a strong thud as the ship rammed into the port. A steward made an announcement from a bullhorn, reminding all passengers to make sure that they had packed all of their belongings. He said anything that was left behind would be thrown away.

The girls could hardly wait to once again feel the solid ground beneath their feet.

While the steerage passengers were waiting for the large ship to slowly maneuver through the East River, a man who had been traveling with the immigrants spoke about the Statue of Liberty. One of his relatives who lived in Manhattan wrote to him and explained that they would be greeted by Lady Liberty when they entered New York Harbor.

"Who is that?" Baizar asked.

"Baizar, don't bother the man," Satenig said.

The man smiled down at the three sisters and said, "She is not bothering me."

"The Statue of Liberty is a symbol of freedom. It was a gift from France to the people of the United States after the Franco-Prussian War during the nineteenth century. The copper statue was sculpted in France in several parts, and each part was shipped separately to the United States. It was then reassembled here on Bedloe's Island. You see, the statue is extremely heavy. It is one hundred and seventy feet high and weighs almost a thousand tons."

"Oh, my, that sounds like a lot of work. How long did it take?" Yestair asked.

"Well, it took more than two years to complete. First, they had to reinforce the foundation and enlarge the island that the Statue of Liberty now stands on. The project was finally finished in 1886."

The girls were fascinated with the story of how the Statue of Liberty became the symbol of freedom in this new and exciting country.

As the ship finally passed by, everyone stood in awe at the sight of the tall, majestic statue of Lady Liberty, holding a lighted torch up to the sky.

Many people were openly sobbing as they sailed past the Statue of Liberty. Everyone realized that the beautiful statue was welcoming them to their new home, "the land of the free."

Hundreds of passengers were waiting on the deck, and were anxious to disembark. The immigrants from steerage were told that they would have to wait until the first-class and the second-class passengers were off the ship.

The ship was almost empty, and it was time for the people who had been in steerage to disembark. The three nervous sisters walked down the gangplank together.

The passengers walked to the end of the dock where they boarded a ferry. The boat would take them to the administration building on Ellis Island.

Everyone climbed on board the huge ferry, and soon, they arrived at Ellis Island. When they got off the ferry, the girls paused to look up at the enormous brick building. Four large towers stood at each corner of the building, and three arched windows were above the entrance of the tall double doors.

The immigrants were told that Ellis Island also had to be reinforced and enlarged before the workers could build the massive main building. The island was in the middle of the Hudson River and was originally only a little over three acres in size. But in 1900, it was enlarged to twenty-seven acres. This was a huge undertaking.

Eventually, more buildings were needed to accommodate the millions of immigrants that were coming to the United States each year. They built a total of twenty-two buildings on the island.

Since the enormous New York City subway system was in the process of being constructed, they used the rocks and dirt from the miles and miles of underground tunnels that were being excavated. The builders also used the dirt and the rocks that were dug up from the Holland Tunnel and the Lincoln Tunnel to enlarge Ellis Island.

The new subway trains would run throughout the five boroughs of New York, which included Manhattan, Queens, the Bronx, Brooklyn, and Staten Island. Passengers could ride the trains, and within less than an hour, they would arrive at any one of the five boroughs for the small price of only a nickel.

After the completion of the buildings, Ellis Island became the official processing center for immigrants in 1892. Each day, thousands of people were questioned and had to endure both physical and mental examinations, which often took three to four hours to complete. More than twelve million people passed through Ellis Island before it closed its doors in 1954.

The girls were told that if anyone was found to have any type of infection, he or she would be detained on the island until they were well enough to enter New York City. Unfortunately, some who had more severe, contagious diseases were sent back to their home countries on the next departing ship.

Yestir was fearful as she anticipated her approaching physical examination. The muscles in her body became tense and the more she gave in to that, the more out of control she felt.

Satenig's heart was racing and her palms were sweating. She thought of how *normal* their lives were, while living at the orphanage. The sisters felt very secure and safe there.

Now their world was shaken, once again. They had no control over the events that they were about to experience in the new country. Her emotions fluctuated as she thought of the uncertainty of their future.

The sisters entered the Great Hall and looked around the large room. It was over a 150 feet long and had a domed roof with two walls of floor-to-ceiling arched windows. There were rows of long stalls which were lined with hundreds of immigrants. The girls felt very intimidated. The lines inched along very slowly, and everyone had to wait patiently until they were told to go upstairs for their physical examinations.

The first-class and second-class passengers went through a quick inspection and were then dismissed. The steerage passengers, however, were scrutinized very carefully.

On an average day, between three and five thousand new arrivals from various countries were examined. Everyone was tired and frustrated. The immigrants were instructed to leave their tagged suitcases and packages and then proceed up the stairs to the examination rooms. They obediently followed one another into the room. Each immigrant had a white card pinned to the lapel of their coat with their name, age, country of origin, and the names of any relatives who were living in the United States at that time.

Doctors and nurses in white coats passed by the immigrants. The doctors would circle around and stare at each person, and then they made a mark on the back of the immigrants' coats with white chalk. The medical staff checked for seventeen different diseases.

If they found a problem with one of the immigrants, that person would be marked with a letter. Each symbol meant something that would determine whether the person would or would not be allowed entry into the United States. Those who were crippled were marked with the letter "L" for lame. If someone's scalp looked infested with lice, the doctor would put an "S" on his coat.

An "E" was for eye problems, which the doctors checked by pulling the eyelids back with a metal button hook. In the event that the doctors found trachoma, which caused blindness, that person was immediately rejected and would have to return to his country on the next departing ship.

Anyone who appeared feeble-minded or showed signs of mental illness would be marked with a large "X" denoting the possibility of insanity. Many people were rejected because it was feared that they would most likely become a public charge.

Eventually, a psychiatric hospital was built on the island in which unstable people were placed. There, they were tested, and their behavior watched. Then they were either allowed to enter the United States or they were returned to their country of origin.

The refugees' papers were carefully examined to see if they had a criminal record.

Everyone underwent a thorough examination, including babies and children. They were checked for measles, whooping cough, and streptococcus of the throat.

If someone had one of these diseases, they would be put into a ward in the newly built Marine Hospital. The main hospital had 120 beds, which made it the largest hospital in the nation at that time.

If someone had a cold or some mild illness, that person would have to remain on Ellis Island in the infirmary until he or she was well. When they were reexamined and pronounced healthy, they would then be allowed to enter the country. If the sick patient was very young, the child's mother was allowed to stay with her child in the infirmary until the child was well enough to leave.

Satenig was most concerned about little Baizar since she had a chronic cough from the time she was four years of age. Although it had gotten better in the past year or so, Satenig was afraid that the doctor would hear something in her chest and deny her entry into the United States.

Satenig bent down and whispered to her young sister, "Baizar, listen to me. When the doctor examines you, be very sweet and keep a smile on your face. Show him how happy you are to be here in America."

"OK, I will try to be happy, Satenig", she replied dejectedly.

Because of the many strict rules, Ellis Island was sometimes called "Heartbreak Island" or the "Isle of Tears." Many people were not allowed to enter the country, and they had to return to their old country.

In 1917, a literacy act was passed, one that required every immigrant to read a forty-word passage in his or her native language. The girls were happy that they could read and write in Armenian, and they passed that test with flying colors.

Satenig thought of her father, who would often spend hours teaching his children and examining their homework to make sure that they were diligent in completing their assignments. If they had any problems, their Papa had always been there to help them. After their homework had been satisfactorily completed, Mama would come into the living room, her arms laden with refreshments. There would be cake or cookies, some kind of fruit, and tall glasses of cold milk. The children always looked forward to their "snack time." Oh, how she missed those wonderful moments when the family laughed and enjoyed their evenings together!

By the end of the year in 1918, Ellis Island was extremely overcrowded because of the large influx of the thousands of immigrants who came to America in order to escape the hunger and oppression in their war-torn countries. Many were survivors of the Great War from 1914 through 1918. This was compounded with the large number of Armenians who were coming to the United States, looking for a safer and a better life, after surviving the death marches during the genocide. The United States was a young and growing country and in dire need of skilled or even unskilled laborers as well as many craftsmen.

Finally, after four long and stressful hours, the girls were filled with great emotion when they learned that they had passed all of their examinations.

An inspector took the girls to the "kissing post," which was a wooden column located on the outside of the registry room. The guard explained that it was where the immigrants were greeted by their relatives. He said that there were many tears, hugs, and kisses and that is why they named it the "kissing post."

The sisters laughed at the silly name and swiftly gathered their possessions and walked outside and into the waiting arms of their Aunt Mary and Uncle John. The girls were so happy and excited to have finally arrived in America, and indeed, there were many tears, hugs, and kisses.

"Hello, I am your Aunt Mary, and this is your Uncle John. We are so happy that you have arrived safely!"

We were concerned about the cold weather since it is wintertime here in the United States. Was your crossing of the Atlantic Ocean rough?"

"The water was very choppy, and sometimes it was really bad," said Satenig, "but we were so happy to be coming to America. We just kept our minds on God and knew how blessed we were to have two relatives who cared about us." A lone tear slid down her cheek.

"When the Near East Relief Organization notified us that your Aunt Mary's brother had three children who were living in an orphanage, we were so surprised and happy," Uncle John said as he put his arm around his weeping wife.

"Now come along, children. Let's be on our way to your new home. We have been anxiously waiting for you to come to New York, and we have so much to share with you and many exciting things to show you," Aunt Mary said as she hugged each of her nieces.

Chapter 18
A New Life

As they walked down the streets of New York, the sisters stared in amazement at the sight of the tall skyscrapers surrounding them. Wherever they looked, they saw crowds of people hurrying along the busy streets of New York City. The girls were so captivated by all the activity in the crowded city that they could hardly take it all in. They were overwhelmed by the sights and all the commotion in the city. Life was so simple in the the orphanage.

After they had walked for several blocks, Uncle John stopped at the curb and pointed to a large, shiny black automobile. "Okay, here's my car," he said. "Climb in, everyone, and we'll be on our way."

"Wait! Where are your horses?" Baizar asked.

"This is a motor car. There is a large motor under the hood that takes the place of the horses. That is why it is sometimes called a 'horseless carriage,'" Uncle John explained as he broadly smiled.

"All I have to do is push this button. Then the engine will start up and the car is ready to go."

"You mean it goes all by itself?" she asked. Baizar was frightened by the car but she tried to act bravely.

Satenig put her arm around her little sister as she thought of her young brother, Aram. He was always interested in new and different things and often said that he wanted to be an inventor when he grew up. She became upset when she thought about his lost life and how he would have been thrilled to ride in this new and exciting invention.

"Does the car go by itself?" Baizar repeated.

"Well, yes and no. I have to step on the gas pedal and then steer the automobile into whatever direction I want to go, and the car goes there. You do not need any horses or stables or even oats for that matter," Uncle John said with a laugh. "All I need to do is step on the gas, and off we go!"

It's a wonderful invention, isn't it?"

When he started the engine, a very loud, rumbling noise caused the frightened sisters to jump. They held on tightly to one another as the car started to move. But soon, the girls began to relax and enjoyed the fast ride in their uncle's fancy motor car as they whizzed by hundreds of pedestrians.

Tears filled Satenig's eyes as she thought of the tragic way her brother died and how all his dreams and aspirations died with him.

In a short while, Uncle John brought the car to a halt in front of a three-story brownstone house.

"We're home!" Aunt Mary announced.

It had been such a long time since they all felt the security of a home.

The girls looked up at the stately, three-story brick townhouse, which was attached on either side by an identical brownstone building. The house was enclosed with a black wrought-iron fence and an intricately detailed wrought-iron gate which led up to the entrance. It was the largest house the girls had ever seen. As they walked up the brick steps, they approached a carved wooden door with a large beveled glass window. They peeked inside and were amazed by the elaborate furnishings that were in the large vestibule.

Shyly, the timid sisters walked into a huge hallway and gazed up at the sparkling crystal chandelier that hung from the high-domed ceiling.

Aunt Mary led the girls into the parlor. In the beautifully furnished room, the girls stared at a deeply tufted red velvet couch that had two matching armchairs placed on either side of it.

They then walked into a stylish dining room that contained an elegantly carved wooden table surrounded by twelve high-backed chairs. The walls were covered in a cream-colored silk fabric. A large gold-leafed mirror adorned one wall, and several gilt-framed oil paintings hung on the remaining three walls. The overall affect was stunning.

"I really like your house," Yestair said. "It is so beautiful, and it is attached to the other houses just like our house was in Armenia. We always loved to go up to the roof, and then we would run from one rooftop to the next to play with our friends. It was so much fun. Can we go up to your roof?"

"Oh, no, my dear, we do not do that here in America. We don't like to bother our neighbors. People here like to enjoy their privacy," Aunt Mary quietly answered.

"We have attached houses here in New York because many people like to live close to their jobs and to the many amenities, such as stores, parks, and theaters. For instance, we live on Fifty-Ninth Street here in Manhattan, and my office is on Sixty-Seventh Street, which is only a short distance away."

"Land is at a premium, and it is expensive to build a house here. Since there is not a great deal of land available, the buildings are three and sometimes four stories high, and in this way, one can have a large home on a relatively small piece of property. Since we live so close to one another, everyone tries to respect their need for privacy," Uncle John further explained.

"I never knew that people in America lived in such luxurious homes," Satenig said. She looked down at her old, wrinkled dress and felt embarrassed. She lowered her eyes and stared at the carved plush carpeting beneath her feet.

Aunt Mary looked at the sad young lady and said, "Girls, why don't we go upstairs to the bedrooms. I would like to show you where you will be sleeping."

They walked up a long flight of stairs covered with red carpeting. Aunt Mary opened a door that led to one of the four bedrooms.

In the center of the room, there was a canopy bed. It was covered with a satin bedspread that was decorated with pale pink satin roses. The border of the bedroom wallpaper had the same kind of pink roses that were on the bedspread.

A white dressing table that was trimmed with metallic gold and a matching chair were on the wall opposite the bed. A large beveled-edge mirror completed the lovely look of the room.

Sitting at the head of the bed, and resting on several plush pillows, was a beautiful doll wearing a white organdy dress with pale pink roses sewn onto the bodice. The room was every young girl's dream of a perfect bedroom.

Running over to the bed, Baizar cried, "Oh, look at the beautiful doll! May I hold her please, Aunt Mary?"

"Of course you can, sweetheart. Not only can you hold her, but she is yours to keep. There is a doll waiting for each of you in your very own bedroom. It is a small 'welcome home' gift."

Suddenly, appearing from nowhere, a large angora cat casually walked into the bedroom. Aunt Mary turned and said, "What are you doing in here? You know you are not allowed to be upstairs. Now shoo. Go back downstairs!"

As she stared at the beautiful cat, Baizar asked, "What is her name?"

"Her name is Snowball. She is a good girl, but at times, she is naughty when she jumps on the bed and begins to claw at the bedspread."

"Oh, please, Aunt Mary, can she stay in here with me. I promise I will scold her if she scratches the bedspread. I really like her, and I think she likes me. Look, see how she is rubbing against my legs!"

Aunt Mary smiled, "All right, I will allow her to stay for a while, but if she starts to claw the rug or the bedspread, out she goes!"

"Oh, thank you so much! I never had a pet before and I know I can train her," Baizar squealed.

"All right, little one, now come along. Let me introduce you to my maid, Takoohi. She is also Armenian, so you may talk to her about any of your needs, and she will be more than happy to assist you in any way she can."

Takoohi was a short, rotund lady who had a big smile on her face.

"I have a new dress for each of you that your aunt and uncle have purchased." She walked over to a large closet and held up three dresses.

Satenig picked up her bundle of clothing and said, "We have another dress in here that we can wear."

Aunt Mary said, "Now wouldn't it be nice to wear a pretty new dress?"

She held up a lovely satin dress for Satenig. Yestair's dress was a soft green-and-white plaid with a dark green sash.

Baizar smiled when she saw the dress that was chosen for her. It was a pink organdy dress with layers of ruffles that cascaded down to the hem.

"Oh, you don't have to give us new dresses. We can wear one of these," Satenig said as she opened her bundle of clothing.

When she held up one of the dresses, a dead cockroach fell to the floor.

Aunt Mary screamed, "Oh, no, no, no! We must get rid of these old clothes!"

Trying to regain some self-control, she quietly said, "Girls, you are now in a new country, so you will need new clothing. Isn't that right?"

The girls numbly nodded in agreement.

"Takoohi, take these clothes down to the dumpster right away. Then give the girls a bath and help them into their new dresses. If they do not fit properly, you may have to make a few adjustments."

As she turned toward the sisters, Aunt Mary said, "When you are ready, come downstairs, and we will have lunch." She gave them a weak smile, turned around, and walked quickly down the stairs.

After she left, Takoohi led the girls into a tiled bathroom. They were mesmerized by the hot and cold running water, which flowed from the chrome faucets into a white porcelain sink. They saw a toilet that had a long chain hanging from a wooden tank. The girls took turns pulling on the chain and laughed as they watched the water whirling down the bowl.

The maid looked annoyed and said, "That is not a toy. You should only pull the chain when you use the toilet."

The girls were embarrassed and nodded their heads in agreement.

Takoohi filled a large bathtub with warm water into which she added some sweet-smelling soap. When she was finally alone, Satenig slipped into the clean water and enjoyed the most luxurious bath she had ever had in her life.

After the girls finished their baths, they felt wonderful. They loved all the modern conveniences in their new home.

Takoohi helped to dress the girls. She carefully combed their tangled hair and then tucked a pretty ribbon into their clean, dried tresses. She made a few adjustments to each of the hems of their dresses, and then when she was finished, the maid said, "Come and look at yourselves in the mirror and see how beautiful you look."

The girls were excited as they twirled around from side to side. They stared at themselves in the mirror and looked at their dresses from all different angles. They hugged one another and laughed happily.

Little Baizar cried, "Oh, my! I look just like a princess!"

Her sisters smiled. "Baizar, you look just like one of those pretty dolls that are sitting on our beds," said Satenig, with a happy smile on her face.

Satenig thought it was like a dream come true. How fortunate they were to be living in a house like this. The Lord had answered their prayers and had given them more than they could ever have hoped or prayed for.

When they went downstairs, the girls saw that the dining room table was laden with so much food that they thought their aunt and uncle were having company. There was a large array of Armenian food—more than they had seen in many years. The dining room table was covered with a white-and-gold-striped linen tablecloth with matching napkins. The fine porcelain china was also white with a gold rim. A large platter was filled with their favorite grape-leaf sarma, freshly baked lavoush bread, and a green salad. Next to each girl's plate was a glass of chocolate milk.

They ate heartily, and near the end of the meal, the cook brought out a crystal bowl filled with fresh fruit like apples, oranges, bananas, and a huge bunch of red grapes.

Aunt Mary noticed that the girls were staring at the fruit bowl, so she said, "Go ahead and take whatever you like. Now don't be shy. This is your new home, and you may eat whatever you like, okay?" She pushed the bowl closer to the children.

Yestair took a large banana and bit into it. She squeezed her eyes shut and cried, "Ugh, this tastes awful! I don't like b-b-bananas!"

Aunt Mary and Uncle John burst into laughter.

Aunt Mary said, "Oh, my dear girl, you must *peel* the banana before you eat it. The fruit is inside." She quickly peeled the banana and handed it back to Yestair.

After she took a tiny bite, Yestair smiled and said, "Oh, this tastes really good!" She quickly devoured the fruit and loudly exclaimed, "I *love* bananas!"

Everyone laughed uproariously.

After lunch, Uncle John said, "Now are you ready to take a walk and see some of the sights in our beautiful city?"

The girls eagerly nodded their heads.

"Okay, I'll give you the fifty-cent tour of Manhattan."

Satenig frowned. "Oh, Uncle John, I don't think we can go. We do not have any money."

Again Aunt Mary and Uncle John looked at one another and smiled. Uncle John hugged the sad child.

"Don't worry, my little dears. That is only an expression. There is no charge to see Manhattan. It is free to anyone who wants to see this great city of ours. I am so sorry. I was trying to make a silly joke," he said.

"You'll have to get used to your Uncle John. He always likes to joke around. Now get your coats and let's go on that tour!" Aunt Mary shouted happily.

When they walked outside, Baizar looked around. "Where's your motor car, Uncle John? I want to take another ride, and let's go really fast this time, okay?"

"No, sweetheart, we will be taking a walking tour. Everything is close by, and it's a beautiful, sunny day and we need the exercise. So let's hold hands and head toward Central Park, which is only a few blocks from here," Uncle John replied.

When they saw the enormous park, the girls ran to look at the lake that was in the center of the park.

"This is going to be the biggest park in Manhattan,"' Uncle John said.

"It is being expanded now, and when it is completed, the park will extend from Fifty-Seventh Street, where we are standing right now up, to 110th Street. It will be a place for the people who work in Manhattan to come and relax after a long, hard day at the office. Also, there is the Museum of Natural History just a few blocks from here. They have real stuffed animals, birds, and reptiles from all over the world. There is a large skeleton of a dinosaur in the main entrance of the museum. It is the biggest and best museum in the world. They also have a big carousel in Central Park for people to ride on."

"What is a carousel, Uncle John?" asked Baizar.

"Why, Baizar, it's the most wonderful thing. It has a wooden platform that goes around and around as the music plays. There are many different kinds of animals on the carousel, and each of you can sit on either a horse or a lion or any animal of your choice and go for a ride. It will be a lot of fun. Just you wait and see!"

Confused, Baizar asked, "Are the animals big? Do they bite?"

"No, no, dear, they are wooden animals painted in pretty colors, and they move up and down while the music plays. The carousel keeps going in circles until the music stops. And then it's time to climb off the animals, and that is the end of the ride. I think you will enjoy it. Would you like to ride on the carousel?"

Still uncertain, Baizar looked at her older sisters. "What do you think? Should we go for a ride?", she cautiously asked.

"Yes, it sounds like fun," Satenig replied. "Let's try it! I'm sure Aunt Mary and Uncle John would not allow us to go on the carousel if it was a dangerous thing to do."

As they neared the large carousel, the girls grew excited and could not wait for the ride to begin. Satenig and Baizar climbed on two gaily colored horses, while Yestair climbed upon an elephant. The music started, and they began to squeal and laugh as they rode around and around on the colorful merry-go-round.

Aunt Mary and Uncle John laughed and waved at the happy girls every time they rode by them. Satenig thought her aunt and uncle were having as much fun as they were. Uncle John had been right. It was more fun than anything they had experienced in a very long time.

When the ride ended, Uncle John suggested that they go to an ice-cream parlor for some cool refreshments. They entered a small store filled with sweet, mouth-watering aromas. After they seated themselves at a long, marble-topped counter, the girls marveled at the large display of treats.

"What would you like? They have ice-cream cones, ice-cream sodas, and decadent sundaes," Aunt Mary suggested.

The girls decided on ice-cream sodas. Satenig ordered a "black-and-white" soda, and Yestair ordered a strawberry soda.

Baizar said, "I would like to have a 'decadent' sundae please." Although she had no idea what a decadent sundae was, Baizar was always the adventurous one in the family. Uncle John and Aunt Mary laughed and thought how sweet and innocent their nieces were.

Everything the children said or did was absolutely delightful to them. It was a new experience for the childless couple, and they were thoroughly enjoying being a "mom" and "dad" to the girls and watching their reactions to all the new and different experiences that were taking place in their young lives.

Uncle John said, “I think I’ll have a New York egg cream.”

“Ugh, what is that? Does it have an egg in the soda?” Baizar asked, making a face.

“Oh, no, It’s just a funny name, but it is only milk, seltzer, and a little bit of chocolate syrup,” Aunt Mary replied. “Uncle John and I like egg creams because they are not fattening and we have to watch our weight.”

As they walked back home, Satenig thought how blessed they were to be living in such an exciting and wonderful country as America.

Chapter 19

Discoveries

Uncle John was a dentist and had a lucrative practice. Unfortunately, there was a void in his and Aunt Mary's life. Since they were unable to have children, they were delighted to have these sweet girls living with them now.

When the girls had arrived, Aunt Mary was happy, and yet a little apprehensive. She knew very little about the needs of three young children, especially knowing the horror and the loss that these little ones had experienced during the past few years. She was apprehensive about the responsibility of taking care of these fragile children. Mary prayed for help from the Lord to cope with the myriad of problems that she faced each day and knew only He could help her to cope with this dire situation.

Aunt Mary and Uncle John were concerned with the welfare of their traumatized, young nieces. They attempted to fill their lives with many new and different experiences. It not only familiarized the girls with an entirely new lifestyle, but it also kept their minds focused on the present and not on the past. They tried to keep the girls busy every weekend. They showed the children how life was in a large metropolitan city.

Since it was only three weeks before the Christmas holiday, Aunt Mary and Uncle John thought that the girls would enjoy visiting Macy's to see the gaily decorated department store. Uncle John told that Macy's was the largest department store in New York City, and because Christmas was only a few short weeks away, they were going to visit Santa Claus.

"Would you like to go and speak to Santa Claus?" Aunt Mary asked Baizar with a smile.

"What is a Santa Claus?" Baizar asked.

"Well, Santa Claus is a jolly old man who will ask you what you would like to have for Christmas. Then you can tell Santa what you want. If you are a very good little girl, you may get what you asked for. When you wake up on Christmas morning, you will find a present under a large Christmas tree," Uncle John replied.

"Oh, that sounds like fun! Can we go now, Uncle John?" exclaimed Baizar.

"Well, we can't go today because I have to go to work, but perhaps we can visit Santa next Saturday. Would that be okay with you?" Uncle John asked with a big grin on his face.

Disappointed, Baizar lowered her head and stared down at the floor.

"Oh, I guess so. Can't you just tell your patients that you can't work on Saturday because you have something very important to do on that day?"

The young child was attempting to forget the past with all the daily struggles that she and her sisters had to endure. In her young mind, she wanted to keep busy so the bad feelings would go away. Baizar turned away and sat on the couch with her head hung low.

Aunt Mary's heart went out to the sad little girl.

"If your uncle doesn't have any patients next Saturday, we will make the trip to Macy's," Aunt Mary promised.

"In the meantime, you will have some time to think about what you would like Santa Claus to bring you on Christmas morning."

"Oh, I already know what I want!" Baizar replied.

"I would like to have a small baby doll so that my beautiful big doll will have a friend. Then she will not feel lonely ever again!"

That poignant remark touched her aunt and uncle's heart, and they immediately decided that they would purchase a baby doll for the child. Aunt Mary thought a tiny crib, some diapers, a small baby bottle, and of course, a few changes of clothing for the baby would make little Baizar a "happy little mommy" on Christmas morning.

Finally the big day arrived, and the girls dressed and went downstairs to the kitchen, where Aunt Mary and Uncle John were just finishing their breakfast.

"Good morning, children. Come sit down and eat your breakfast. We will be leaving soon, and it will be a very busy day, so you need some nourishing food to sustain you," Aunt Mary said.

The girls sat down and ate their bacon and eggs with a slice of buttered toast and a cold glass of freshly squeezed orange juice. They were then served a cup of hot chocolate with some chocolate chip cookies, which they gulped down noisily.

"Okay, that was good! Now can we leave and go see Santa Claus?" asked Baizar.

Uncle John smiled and said, "Get your hats and coats and a warm pair of gloves because it is very cold outside."

The girls quickly dressed and waited for Uncle John to start the automobile. It took several minutes for the car to warm up due to the extremely cold weather. When the car was warm and cozy, Uncle John told the family to climb in. They began their trip downtown.

Macy's was located at Herald Square and Thirty-Fourth Street. As their uncle drove the automobile, he explained that Mr. R. H. Macy had opened a small store in 1862. The store became so successful that he had to enlarge the establishment several times. In 1910, it became the largest department store in the entire world.

"Mr. Macy was the first store owner to hire a 'live' Santa Claus to talk to the many children who accompanied their parents to the store. That was a very good business move because thousands of parents with their children in tow visit the massive store and business is now booming," Uncle John explained.

When they arrived at their destination, their uncle drove around until he finally found a parking space several blocks away from the store. When they approached Macy's, the girls stared in amazement at the beautifully decorated windows. Inside one of the windows, there was an enormous Christmas tree that was covered with hundreds of colored twinkling lights. A large illuminated star shone from the top of the tree.

The girls were in awe as they stared at the colorfully wrapped presents under the tree. They stood motionless, as they heard the sound of Christmas carols sung by the employees as the customers were entering the store. They had never witnessed anything as enchanting as the window displays at Macy's, and they were anxious to go and see Santa Claus.

The three sisters waited in a long line and watched intently as Santa quietly spoke to each boy and girl. They listened as he asked each child what he or she wanted for Christmas, and then he presented them with a red-and-white-striped candy cane and a small toy as a parting memento of their visit with "Old St. Nick."

Finally, it was Baizar's turn to speak to Santa Claus. "Santa" noticed how nervous the small girl appeared, so he gently picked Baizar up and sat her on his lap.

"Ho, ho, ho, and what is your name, little girl?" Santa asked.

Baizar answered with her heavy Armenian accent. "My name is Baizar, Santo, and I want a baby."

Santa attempted to keep a straight face as he asked the youngster if she had been a good girl.

Baizar stared at the bearded man, nodded her head, grabbed the candy cane and toy from Santa's hand, and jumped off his lap.

Santa Claus laughed and called out, "You're welcome!" as he watched the tiny girl run away.

Satenig and Yestair were a little confused and could not understand what Santa Claus was laughing about, so they made their requests quickly and left to find their little sister.

Aunt Mary and Uncle John were tittering as they watched the amusing scene of Santa Claus and the funny little foreign child who grabbed his candy cane and toy and ran away without even a "thank you, Santa."

After they rounded up their nieces, Aunt Mary took the girls to the children's clothing department while Uncle John left for the men's suit department. Aunt Mary had the girls try on several dresses and some skirts and blouses. She watched and listened to the sisters' reactions and their various comments about the clothing. After an hour or so, Aunt Mary had a better idea of the likes and dislikes of each child, which would help make her Christmas shopping easier.

In a short while, Uncle John returned to the children's department, toting a large Macy's shopping bag. He was finished with his shopping and suggested that they get something to eat. After everyone was safely in the automobile, Uncle John announced, "I feel like having a hot dog and an orangeade drink. Nathan's is famous for their hot dogs."

"What do you mean by a 'hot dog,' Uncle John?" asked Yestair.

"How can a dog be hot? It is freezing cold outside!"

Throwing his head back, Uncle John laughed.

"A hot dog is tasty sausage that is shaped like a long roll. It is placed in a bun, and it is topped with mustard and sauerkraut."

"Yum, it is so tasty! I can eat two or three hot dogs all by myself," he said.

When they arrived at Nathan's, Aunt Mary and Uncle John walked to a counter and ordered a large tray of Nathan's famous hot dogs and five large drinks of orangeade. The girls ate heartily and loved the strange but delicious food.

Upon their return to the house, Aunt Mary asked her nieces if they had enjoyed the day. The girls all began to speak at the same time about how much fun they had at Macy's. They also loved the odd taste of the hot dogs, which was so different from the Armenian food that they were familiar with.

As everyone was speaking about the fun and the exciting new adventures they were experiencing in Manhattan, Satenig became very quiet, and she seemed to be lost in thought. She had thoroughly enjoyed the day, yet she somehow felt guilty that she and her sisters were having so much fun. She missed her family so terribly, that at times, in the midst of all the joviality; she would at times become melancholy.

Aunt Mary looked at her and saw that Satenig appeared to be a little melancholy. She walked over to her niece and put her arm around her.

"How are you doing, Satenig? You seem a little tired. Are you feeling all right?"

Satenig nodded. "I'm fine. I am just a little down when I think how much my younger sister and brother would have enjoyed this wonderful day. It is so unfair that innocent children have missed so much of life because of the selfish cruelty of men. They didn't deserve to die, Aunt Mary. My brother, Aram, was such a happy-go-lucky little boy. He loved any new adventure, and if he had lived, he would have loved to have taken part in today's fun at Macy's. It just breaks my heart and—"

When Aunt Mary saw copious tears streaming down Satenig's cheeks, she hugged her niece to her bosom. "I know what a terrible ordeal you girls have gone through, but you must be thankful that our Lord has brought you through the fire. You must always remember that your dear family is home with our heavenly Father."

"Oh, I know we have been blessed. We are so fortunate to have you and Uncle John providing a home for us. I'm also so thankful for the wonderful missionaries who took good care of us at the orphanage."

Satenig wiped her tears with the back of her hand. "Thank you, Aunt Mary. You and Uncle John have been so kind and wonderful to us, and we do love and appreciate both of you so very much."

"Well, we are happy to help in any way we can. I know my brother, Paul, was a warm and loving father to his children. Even as a child, he was a serious-minded young man with a God-given talent as an artist.

Many times, he would sit and sketch detailed scenes that most adults were incapable of doing. He was a brilliant and talented man, and I miss him terribly," Aunt Mary said as her eyes filled with tears.

Trying to compose herself, Aunt Mary smiled. "I have a great idea! How about we girls go on a shopping spree on Monday! Would you like that? It will be just the four of us since your Uncle John will be working at the office. We will spend the entire day shopping until our bags are filled with lots of newfound treasures. Later, we can go out to eat at any restaurant of your choice. It will be a fun-filled day, I promise you."

Now that the girls were adjusting to their new environment in New York, Aunt Mary decided that it was time to make plans for their education and their future.

Chapter 20

New York

THE VIBRANT ATMOSPHERE OF THE city was exhilarating, although at times, they longed for the quiet days in their small village. The sisters loved living in New York. Satenig remembered the many times that she had stood in awe as she gazed upon the magnificent grandeur of Mount Ararat. Now as she looked up, all she could see were man-made skyscrapers that were sprouting up throughout the city.

One spring day as Satenig and Uncle John drove passed the Woolworth Building, he told her that it was the tallest building in the world. He stopped the car, and they tilted their heads and looked up at the soaring structure before them. It was forty-seven stories high.

Satenig stared and asked, "How can anyone walk up all those steps?"

"Years ago, a man named Elisha Otis invented the elevator," Uncle John replied.

"What is an elevator?" Satenig asked.

"It is a motorized, enclosed cabin that can move from one floor to the next floor. In this way, the businessmen who work in these tall buildings can go to the top without having to walk up hundreds of steps," explained Uncle John.

Again, Satenig marveled at the magnificence of the largest metropolitan area in the United States. The city was divided into five boroughs. Each borough of New York was larger than most towns were in the United States.

"The City," as many locals referred to it, was teeming with people. Thousands of foreigners were migrating there from various countries throughout the world. Most of the immigrants left the "old country," seeking employment opportunities and a new and better way of life in America.

Therefore, New York was often called the "melting pot" because of the countless, diverse cultural groups of people that were living there. During the hot and humid summer months, one could quickly identify the ethnic backgrounds by the odiferous aromas that emanated from the open windows of the apartments in the overcrowded tenements.

One knew that the pungent smell of tomato sauce was indigenous to Italian cooking. Bratwurst was a staple for the Germans. The Greeks and Armenians had a distinct scent from the many strong spices and herbs that were used in preparing their traditional cuisine.

Lamb was a staple in an Armenian home. The aroma of a leg of lamb baking in the oven was a time-honored tradition. Lahmajoon was a favorite treat for the Armenians. This meat pie was seasoned with ground lamb, tomatoes, cumin, coriander, and allspice and then baked on bread dough.

The people in each ethnic group lived close to one another because it was easier to converse in their native tongue. They enjoyed sharing stories about how life was in their former countries. The Jewish and Italian immigrants lived in lower Manhattan. Many of the Irish, Germans, Greeks, and Armenians resided in midtown Manhattan.

The immigrants had few modern skills. They had to take any job that they could find. Many worked in factories called "sweatshops" because there was very little ventilation in the hot, almost windowless, brick buildings. The conditions were deplorable, but the workers were thankful to even have a job.

The years went by quickly as the girls became more involved in many new activities. The sisters were becoming more content, and their lives were full.

Aunt Mary and Uncle John were kind and concerned substitute parents, although they could not completely fill the void in the girls' fragmented lives. The sisters still missed their beloved family and their life as it had been before the tragic events of the genocide. They continually read and heard about the devastation that was still occurring in their war-torn country. The newspapers were filled with all the gruesome details. It was estimated that over a million and a half men, women, and children had perished from the mass murders and from starvation when they were forced to walk through the deserts without any food or water. Thus, the expression, "the starving Armenians" became a commonly used phrase whenever someone was hungry and in need for food.

When the girls observed the squalid conditions in the noisy and cramped quarters of the tenement buildings in lower Manhattan, they were thankful for their two caring guardians.

One day, Aunt Mary approached her nieces and asked them to sit down so that she could have a talk with them. The girls immediately grew concerned. Yestair frowned and worried that perhaps she or one of her sisters had done something wrong. Aunt Mary noticed that her niece was nervously twisting and untwisting a handkerchief that she held in her hand.

When she saw the worried looks on her nieces' solemn faces, Aunt Mary smiled. "Please do not be upset. There is nothing wrong. I just wanted to let you know about a private school just a few miles from our house. It is a bilingual school where teachers are fluent in both English and Armenian. Your uncle and I think it would be very beneficial for you to learn how to read and write in English. Classes will begin next month, and we want you to seriously consider attending this school. Since your permanent home is now here in America, I think it would be wise for you to think about your future."

"We have also thought about your attending the Armenian Apostolic Church on Twenty-Ninth Street. The church provides many activities for young people," added Aunt Mary.

"So what do you think? I have done a lot of talking. I want you to think about what I've said and be honest with me. Tell me if you have any doubts or questions, and we will discuss them together as a family."

After a short discussion, the girls agreed that they needed some direction in their lives, and the benefit of attending school seemed like an excellent idea.

The sisters were anxious for school to begin. At first, they were self-conscious and shy, but soon, they adjusted to their new environment. Eventually, the girls learned to speak English, although not fluently but well enough to converse with their newly found American friends at school. They looked forward to going to school each day.

Many of their classmates went to the same church as they did, and soon, the sisters were involved in the church activities. The girls particularly enjoyed the Hantes get-togethers, which featured Armenian musicians who played music and songs from the old country. These get-togethers were followed by a huge, authentic Armenian buffet. The girls also attended arts and crafts classes and they enjoyed meeting other children of their own age. It was here that they formed lasting friendships with their Christian friends.

When Satenig was seventeen years old, she began to work in a women's dress factory that produced very stylish clothing. During the hot, humid days, she would come home completely exhausted after she had worked in the sweltering factory for eight or nine hours. The building had only a few small windows and only three or four fans, which were inadequate to cool the entire work area.

Satenig enjoyed sewing, and she began to design and make dresses for herself and her two sisters.She even made a lovely summer dress for her Aunt Mary, who was impressed with the natural talent that her niece had in creating a garment that was an "original" and was not the same style as all of the other dresses that one found in a department store.

Occasionally, when Satenig had time off from work, she would accompany her uncle on some errands. She loved riding in his luxurious automobile and enjoyed looking at the crowds of people as they rushed by along the streets of New York.

One day, Uncle John asked her if she would like to take a ride downtown. Of course, she immediately said she would love to go with him. When they arrived at a small tailor shop in downtown Manhattan, Uncle John pulled up in front of the store.

"I need to have two of my suits dry-cleaned and pressed. Do you want to come inside, or would you rather wait for me in the car?" he asked.

"I'll go with you, Uncle John," Satenig replied. "It's rather warm here in the car."

When they walked into the shop, they were greeted by the owner, Paul Nalbandian. Uncle John introduced him to his niece.

Satenig stared at the handsome and personable young man, who warmly smiled and shook her hand. They spoke for a while, and Paul informed them that the suits would be ready the following week. At that very moment, Satenig decided that she would most definitely accompany her uncle when he returned to pick up his newly cleaned suits.

Satenig counted the days until it was time to return to the small tailor shop. When she and Uncle John walked into the store, Paul warmly greeted them and smiled broadly at the young woman. Satenig's heart skipped a beat.

When they were ready to leave, Paul walked over to Satenig and asked if she would like to join him for dinner. Surprised but happy, she smiled shyly and nodded her head in agreement.

Before long, Paul and Satenig began to date regularly. She loved everything about him, and he felt the same way about her. Paul took her to see a Broadway play, and Satenig loved the live performance. After the show, they walked to a nearby restaurant for a bite to eat.

As Satenig was enjoying her meal, she looked up at Paul and saw him staring at her with a slight smile on his face.

"Is something wrong, Paul?" Satenig asked. "You have an odd look on your face."

“No, there is nothing wrong, but something is very right,” he replied. “I love you, and I think about you all the time. I hope you feel the same way about me.”

“I would like to ask you a question. Would you consider marrying me, Satenig?”

Satenig sat very still and thought for a moment.

Looking deeply into his blue eyes, she whispered, “I feel the same as you do, Paul, but I am struggling with the fact that if I marry at this time, my sisters may have a set-back. We have been through some harrowing experiences in the past and I thank the Lord that my sisters seem to be adjusting fairly well through all the struggles and changes in their young lives. I don’t know what would happen if I were to marry at this time.”

She stopped, and inhaled deeply and said, “I truly love you, Paul, but I hope you can understand my being hesitant about getting married at this time.”

Paul reached over and held Satenig’s hand. “Darling, I completely understand that you are concerned about your siblings but they are stronger than you think. After all the terrible times that they have had in the past, I think they are remarkably strong young ladies. Sure they have their times of sadness and despair but all children go through change during their growing years. Please do not worry about your sisters. Remember, we will always be there for them, if for any reason they were having a problem or were struggling with a situation.”

Satenig smiled at Paul and knew why she loved this man so very much. Satenig looked at Paul adoringly. She knew what she wanted to say, but she thought for a moment and said, “My aunt and uncle have been so good to me, and out of respect, I think you should speak to them first before I can give you an answer, Paul.”

When Satenig returned home, she immediately told her Aunt Mary about the marriage proposal from Paul. Mary was a little surprised. Paul was a thirty-eight-year-old man, and she was not sure if the nearly twenty-year age difference in age would be a favorable match for her niece.

"Why don't you ask Paul to come to dinner on Saturday night? I'm sure your Uncle John will want to speak to him," suggested Aunt Mary.

Paul eagerly accepted the dinner invitation and arrived promptly. He presented a large bouquet of roses to the hostess. He was sporting a three-piece dark blue suit with a matching fedora.

When Satenig saw him, she was so happy, and she hoped that everything would turn out favorably.

After dinner, Uncle John and Paul retired to his study, and the two men spoke about the future plans that Paul had made. He told Uncle John that he was deeply in love with his niece. He said he had a very prosperous business and would be able to provide Satenig with the kind of lifestyle that she so richly deserved. Then Paul reached into his vest pocket and showed Uncle John the beautiful, square-cut diamond engagement ring that he intended to give to his future wife, if it met with their approval.

Uncle John excused himself and went into the living room to speak to his wife. After a fifteen-minute discussion, they both agreed that it was time for Satenig to have some true happiness in her life.

Uncle John and Aunt Mary returned to the study with their anxious niece in tow. Uncle John walked over to Paul who was sitting on the edge of his seat. He placed Satenig's hand in Paul's, and he and his wife gave them their blessing.

On September 9, 1922, Paul and Satenig were married in the Armenian Apostolic Church. It was a small but lovely ceremony. Satenig was a beautiful bride in her elegant wedding gown which she had designed and sewn by hand. It was an unusual and elegant creation. She also made the gowns which her two beloved sisters wore as her maid of honor and bridesmaid.

After a short honeymoon to Niagara Falls, the newlyweds moved into a six-story high-rise apartment building in upper Manhattan.

Satenig continued to produce exclusive, one-of-a-kind dresses and suits for many of her husband's customers. Soon word got around about the unique clothing that Satenig designed and made, and the demand quickly grew for her chic, custom-made creations.

Eventually, the happy couple had three children, Agnes, Edward, and Angel. Satenig's life was full, and her dream had finally come true.

Yestair and Baizar continued to live with their aunt and uncle on Fifty-Seventh Street. As Satenig's business grew, she "hired" her two sisters as her assistants. The girls were happy because they had greatly missed their older sister since she had married. They worked well together, and business was booming.

Two years later, Yestair married and moved to the Bronx. Her husband was employed by the New York Highlanders, which ultimately became the New York Yankees. Yestair suffered the loss of many miscarriages but finally gave birth to a sweet little boy named Armen.

In 1935, Baizar met her future husband, who was a sales representative for fabric, trims, and notions at Paul's tailor shop. They were married two years later and moved to the suburbs of northern New Jersey. In 1941, their only son, Aram, was born.

Chapter 21
Church Meeting

In April 1950, the three sisters and their spouses attended a special church service commemorating the thirty-fifth anniversary of the 1915 Armenian genocide. The church was filled to capacity. Church members had been notified that a number of missing relatives who were presumed to be dead were in fact alive and living in other countries.

The pastor preached a poignant message in remembrance of the men, women, and children who had lost their lives in the first genocide of the twentieth century.

After he had finished preaching, the pastor announced that Mr. Armen Ohanian from the Near East Relief Organization would be speaking about the missing survivors of the genocide.

Mr. Ohanian stood up and began to explain that for many years since the massacre, thousands of people who had lost relatives had been making inquiries about their deceased family members. A committee had been formed in an attempt to locate survivors of the genocide. They found many Armenians who were now living in different countries throughout the Middle East. Some were living in Syria, Lebanon, Egypt, and Israel.

Mr. Ohanian spoke of the difficulty in attempting to piece together what little information they had. Since there was no list of names to begin with, it had taken them many years of research to verify the information. Through years of investigation, they now had compiled a lengthy list of names of individuals who had survived the genocide.

Mr. Ohanian held up a thick packet of paper and said, "I am holding in my hand a list of the names of individuals that we have located in the Middle East and surrounding countries. We have all of the names and addresses of the survivors. My colleague and I will be downstairs in the fellowship hall after the service, and we will be more than happy to answer any questions that you may have concerning a missing relative. So please take a few minutes to meet with us. Perhaps you will be able to reconnect with a long-lost relative."

Satenig and Yestair stared at one another with stunned looks on their faces. "Let's go downstairs and ask some questions about Aznif! We really don't know if Aznif died or if by some miracle that she could have survived. Wouldn't it be an answer to prayer if we could find our sister after all these years?" Satenig asked excitedly.

When they reached the fellowship hall, Mr. Ohanian and his assistant were sitting at a long table with a stack of paperwork in front of them. Many people were crowding around the table, and everyone was asking questions at the same time.

Mr. Ohanian held up his hand and said, "I know you are all anxious to find out about a missing loved one. I believe it would be more expedient if we read the names of the survivors, which are listed alphabetically by their last names."

The assistant began to read the names aloud, and as he reached the letter "K," the sisters listened intently for Aznif's name. As he began to read *Kashagian*, *Kavakian*, and then *Kerbajian*, Satenig's hand flew to her chest, and she whispered, "Could it be—"

The man then said, "Aznif."

The three sisters could not believe it.

Satenig held onto Yestair and began to weep.

"Could it be *our* beloved sister and not someone else?"

They approached Mr. Ohanian and asked him how they could contact their missing sister. He looked through a large ledger until he located Aznif's name and her current address in Beirut, Lebanon. Then he wrote down the information on a sheet of paper and handed it to Satenig.

Mr. Ohanian suggested that they write to her and ask some pertinent questions, such as her date of birth, her parents' names, and where she was born.

Mr. Ohanian gave them his business card and told them to contact his office, if in fact the woman turned out to be their sister. He and the members of his staff would then help them fill out the necessary papers and make arrangements for Aznif to come to the United States.

The excited sisters could hardly contain themselves. They tightly hugged one another and their husbands as tears poured down their faces.

When she got home, Satenig immediately began to compose a letter to Aznif. She wrote that she and her two sisters, Yestair and Baizar, were now living in the United States. She asked Aznif to write back with the date of her birth, the town she was born in, and most importantly, her parents' names.

She also asked Aznif how many siblings she had and what their names were.

Satenig also thought it was a good idea to mention the time in their past when their brother, Aram had played a trick on Mama. He bit into a juicy, red pomagranet and ran to Mama. He told her that he had knocked out his tooth and was bleeding. She remembered how mad Papa was by Aram's childess prank. He punished Aram and made him apologize to Mama for his thoughtlessness.

Satenig smiled as she reread the letter and then mailed the letter out immediately. She prayed and hoped for a quick and positive response.

When Aznif received the letter, she was in a complete state of shock. She had resigned herself to the life she had in Beirut as a live-in maid. At the age of forty-two, her life was quiet and uneventful. Of course, she missed her family and often felt sad and lonely, but she was content with the job she had held with the Sarkisian family for the last twenty years.

Before she had joined them, Aznif had lived with three other Armenian families and served as a nanny and at times as a housekeeper or maid.

Aznif asked Mr. Sarkisian, who was an attorney, what she should do. He advised her to send a letter stating that she was indeed their sister and how happy she was to know that they were alive and well. He helped Aznif compose a letter listing all the required information about her past.

In addition, Aznif had to complete many forms and affidavits and submit them to the proper authorities. After almost two years of anxiously waiting for the paperwork to be processed and approved, she received a confirmation letter stating that she was free to go to the United States.

Her sisters asked Aznif to send a recent photo of herself, and in return, they would forward one of themselves. This would allow them to recognize one another when they met.

Satenig, Yestair, and Baizar pooled their money together to purchase a one-way airplane ticket from Beirut to New York for their sister.

With Mr. Sarkisian's assistance, the sisters made arrangements for Aznif to travel to the United States. Her employer said Aznif was a good worker and a wonderful person. He was sorry to lose her, yet he was extremely happy that she would be reunited with her long-lost family.

On a warm, sunny day in June of 1953, Aznif, who was filled with fear and trepidation, boarded a large plane at the Beirut airport. As she timidly walked aboard the plane, she looked around the enormous interior and realized that she did not know where to go. A smiling airline stewardess saw the confused look on her face.

"May I see your boarding pass?" she asked.

Aznif gave her a blank look. "I'm sorry. I don't know if I have a boarding pass," she answered.

The stewardess looked at the distressed woman. She noticed that she was clutching a piece of paper in her hand.

"Oh, you have the boarding pass here in your hand, my dear," replied the stewardess.

Embarrassed, Aznif looked down at the crushed boarding pass and quickly handed it to the stewardess.

"Oh, I am so sorry. I have never been on an airplane. I am a little nervous and confused."

The stewardess smiled and replied, "There is nothing to worry about. Just follow me, and I'll take you to your assigned seat."

She walked toward the back of the plane and sat her next to the window. When the plane's engines started to rev up, Aznif grew tense and prayed fervently for safety. As the plane began to soar up into the sky, Aznif closed her eyes for a moment. When she looked out of the window and saw that she was high above the clouds, she sat back and looked in awe at the beauty of God's creation.

When the stewardess brought a tray of food and a hot cup of coffee, Aznif relaxed and realized that she was actually enjoying the plane ride.

She leaned back and began tatting with her needle and thread. After a very long flight, the airplane finally touched down at LaGuardia Airport in Queens, New York.

As she walked down the steps of the plane, Aznif saw crowds of people welcoming their friends and relatives. Her eyes darted back and forth as she anxiously looked around for her sisters.

Aznif was in a state of panic when she could not find them.

Suddenly, she saw three middle-aged women waving and calling her name.

The sisters were so excited. They had not seen Aznif in thirty-eight years!

They all looked forward to this reunion.

"Aznif, is that you?" Baizar yelled as they all ran toward their sister with outstretched arms.

"This is the moment we have been waiting for since we found out that you had survived and had been living in Beirut," said Satenig.

Suddenly, Satenig stopped talking. She noticed that Aznif was wearing the earrings that Papa had given to their mother on their fifteenth wedding anniversary. When Yestair and Baizar saw Satenig's tears, they remembered that horrific day when their lives had changed forever.

The women hugged and cried as they embraced one another. The four Kerbajian sisters were together once again.

Walking arm in arm, the overjoyed women left the airport and headed for *home.*

Chapter 22

Back to 1965

THERE WAS A DEAD SILENCE at the dinner table. The entire family was speechless. The children and grandchildren were shocked by the brutality and the horror of what their relatives had gone through during the genocide.

Everyone was trying to process the terrible events that their parents and grandparents had endured over fifty years ago. Some of the children were very emotional while others were angry that people could be so cruel to innocent men, women, and children.

"I don't understand why the United States didn't get involved and stop the Turks in their tracks!" Albert firmly said.

Satenig thought for a moment and carefully replied to her grandson.

"Albert, at that time, the United States and many countries throughout Europe were in the midst of a major war. From 1914 to 1918, all eyes were focused on World War I. It is important to remember that the genocide of the Armenians was strategically planned to occur at the same time that all of Europe was deeply enmeshed in a world war. World War I was front-page news, and the reporters concentrated on the thousands of American soldiers who had been wounded or killed. Many of the newspapers in the United States were reporting the plight in the Near East, and the journalists did occasionally write about the Armenians who were literally starving to death."

"The American Red Cross and other organizations did send money, food, and medical supplies to the destitute survivors," Baizar added.

"Wow, I never really understood what the expression 'starving Armenians' really meant."

"Now that I know the significance of that expression, I feel very badly about using it so flippantly," Robert replied.

"I'm sure most people don't understand its true meaning," Satenig told her grandson.

"It is also of great importance for the family to know that our Christian heritage dates back to the days of Noah in the Bible," Satenig interjected.

"Did you know that the Armenians are direct descendants of Noah?"

Young Eddie's ears perked up, and he excitedly yelled, "Wow! You mean the Noah in the Bible who built the Ark?"

"Yes, that Noah," his grandmother softly replied.

"Grandma, the story of Noah's Ark is one of my favorite stories in the Bible!" Eddie said.

"It might be of interest for you to know that one of Noah's grandsons was named Haig, and the name *Haig* means 'Armenian.'

"And your grandmother and your aunts were all born near the base of Mount Ararat," Yestair continued.

"I do remember hearing somewhere that Armenia was the first nation in the world to officially adopt Christianity as its religion. Is that true?" Albert asked.

"Yes, you're absolutely right, Albert."

"I learned so much today, but I still don't understand why you waited so long to tell the family about this terrible tragedy," Steven said.

"It was too painful to talk about it and to relive the events that occurred during that time. After all these years, the massacre is still deeply ingrained in our minds."

"I often wake up at night, remembering the horrors of the past. That is when I ask God to give me the peace and courage to go on," Aznif replied.

"This all occurred a long time ago. After many years of silence, we now understand how important it is for our family to know what actually happened in 1915," Aznif said, as the family nodded their heads in agreement.

"This is the most shocking story that I've ever heard. You should write a book about what happened to our family!" Albert stated emphatically.

And so we did.

Epilogue

The Armenian Empire dates back to the sixth century BC. It was one of the largest and most powerful countries in Asia, stretching from the Mediterranean Sea to the Caspian Sea. Throughout most of its long history, Armenia was invaded by a succession of empires. Because of its vulnerable location, the Armenians were continually attacked by the Greeks, Romans, Persians, and the Byzantine and Ottoman Turks. Many battles were fought throughout the land, destroying an ancient culture that had evolved over four thousand years. Today, the country of Armenia has been reduced to the size of the state of Maryland, and it is located in the Near East, south of Russia and east of Turkey.

Armenia was the cradle of civilization where Noah's Ark was located. Armenians were descendants of Noah, which is the reason Mt. Ararat holds great significance for them. They have considered Ararat as the holiest place in the world and the symbol of their Christianity.

Christianity was brought to Armenia in 43 AD by two apostles of Jesus Christ, Thaddeus and Bartholomew. They travelled throughout the empire, preaching the word of God, and many were converted to Christianity.

Today, in Jerusalem, the walled Old City is divided into four ancient and distinctive cultures: Jewish, Muslim, Christian, and Armenian. The Armenian quarter is represented because of the fact that it was the first nation in the world to adopt Christianity as its state religion.

The atrocities that took place during the Armenian massacre still continue to occur throughout the world today. Genocides have continued to ravish the countries of Bosnia, Rwanda, and Darfur. Many have looked back in horror and said, "Never again!" We cannot sit in social apathy and deny the past.

The world looks upon the genocidal attack against the Jewish people during World War II with horror. Prior to his invasion of Poland, Adolph Hitler gave a speech in 1939 and said, "I have given orders to my death units to exterminate, without pity, all Jewish men, women, and children who are Polish. It is only in this manner that we can acquire the vital territory we need. After all, who speaks today of the annihilation of the Armenians?"

Henry Morgenthau, who was the US ambassador to the Ottoman Empire from 1913 to 1916, wrote the following: "The whole history of the human race contains no such horrible episodes as this. The great massacres and persecutions of the past seem insignificant when compared to the sufferings of the Armenian race in 1915. In that year, two thirds of the Armenian population died by mass execution or by starvation."

This book is based on a true story. Each of the sisters recounted their experiences of what occurred during that time. This poignant tale has remained silent for many years, because it was too painful for the survivors to relive the atrocities that they had witnessed and endured. But they came to realize that it was important for the next generation to *never* forget these crimes against humanity. It is our hope that in a small way, we have given Armenia a voice.

Paul Kerbajian was martyred for his unwavering faith in Jesus Christ. He made a decision early in his life to accept the Lord and His free gift of salvation. Paul's faith remained strong even in times of persecution. This has greatly impacted his family and future generations.

It was "His Choice" to follow the Lord.

That if thou shalt confess with thy mouth the Lord Jesus, and shalt believe in thine heart that God hath raised him from the dead, thou shalt be saved.

Romans 10:9

Wedding picture of Paul Kerbajian and his wife

Aznif Kerbajian in 1953

Prior to reunion with her sisters in New York City

Yestair, Baizar and Satenig Kerbajian

Three sisters who eventually made their way to the United States

And I saw thrones, and they sat upon them, and judgment was given unto them: and I saw the souls of them that were beheaded for the witness of Jesus, and for the word of God, and which had not worshipped the beast, neither his image, neither had received his mark upon their foreheads, or in their hands; and they lived and reigned with Christ a thousand years.

Revelation 20:4-6